DAWN OF THE STORM

A Raina Storm Thriller – Book One

Kim Cresswell

KC Publishing
Ontario, Canada

KC Publishing
London, Ontario Canada

Publisher's Note: This is a work of fiction. Names, characters, places, and incidents are a product of the author's imagination. Locales and public names are sometimes used for atmospheric purposes. Any resemblance to actual people, living or dead, or to businesses, companies, events, institutions, or locales is completely coincidental.

Cover Art © 2018

Ordering Information:
Quantity sales. Special discounts are available on quantity purchases by corporations, associations, and others. For details, contact the publisher at the address above.

Dawn of the Storm/Kim Cresswell. – 1st edition.
ISBN 978-0-9950578-7-6

For Justin, Carla, Porter, and Peyton

In memory of Mary Beech

Death leaves a heartache no one can heal, love leaves
a memory no one can steal.
– From a headstone in Ireland

CHAPTER ONE

Avila Beach, California - November 17th

Umar Sarouk glanced up at the over-sized wall clock in the sterile fifty-by-fifty-foot control room and exhaled a long steady breath. It was six-thirty in the morning, and his twelve-hour shift at Diablo Canyon Nuclear Plant would end in thirty minutes.

After twenty years of marriage, he would not be returning home to his wife and two daughters. There would be no graduations, no weddings to attend, and he wouldn't be celebrating his forty-seventh birthday next week. Nor would he meet his first grandchild due in three months, born to his eldest daughter, Jewel.

Any apprehension for what he was about to do had disappeared months ago, replaced with deep sorrow for the many things in life he would miss. His children. His wife. His friends.

He leaned back in the chair and looked around the horseshoe-shaped room cluttered with vertical panels, bench boards and control switches used to monitor the nuclear reactor's coolant pumps, steam generator, and pressurizer levels. A lifetime of memories flashed, fast-forwarding through his mind, and he held on to each of them like a life preserver.

He knew the time would come when he would be called upon to carry out a mission and he gladly accepted his fate. After he was gone, the experts would argue that he had been 'radicalized' to an unbending ideology; that specific signs were ignored before he'd reached the final plateau. They call it the 'jumping-off point to terror'. But Umar knew they wouldn't uncover any of the typical signs.

He had done everything he had been ordered to do to stay off the FBI's radar, including keeping his thoughts to himself, not once indulging his ideation, beliefs or fears to anyone, not even to his wife. He never lived a life of isolation and never posted messages on social media. More importantly, no one was aware of his link to Al Qaeda. At least, not yet. For the first time in his life, Umar felt whole—that he was part of something greater.

He wrung his hands together and noticed how his stubby fingers trembled slightly. It was almost time. He stood and faced the clock. His legs shook. He clutched the edge of the desk and held his head high.

Six-forty-nine. The calm before the storm.

For over eight months, he had smuggled all the necessary parts he needed into the facility, hiding pieces in his locker, behind the washroom hand dryer, in his lunch, and even in plastic bags submerged in the toilet tanks. As a nuclear engineer, he had access to restricted areas that were usually off limits to many of the employees. Every free moment he had, he secretly assembled the explosive devices and placed each one where he knew they would have the most impact.

Six-fifty-five.

Sweat slid down his forehead and dripped onto the bridge of his nose. He swiped the wetness away with the back of his hand and thought about his wife, Afina, grateful for the many wonderful years they'd had together. She was a good woman. A good mother. She'd never forgive him.

Seven o'clock.

Umar's heart pounded.

The lights flicked off.

The electrical malfunction had originated at the power station a half-mile north. He knew this because it was part of the plan to guarantee his mission was a success.

Two minutes later, the plant's backup diesel generator fired up. The control room lights flickered twice then stayed on. Panic took over, and his breath came out in small bursts of air.

Remember why you're doing this.

A loud boom directly below him sounded like lightning hitting a tree. He swore the tile floor shifted. The vibration from the explosion rippled up through his feet and tunneled through his body. He grabbed the edge of the desk to steady his balance.

The first bomb was meant to disrupt the backup power supply and the cooling system to the nuclear reactors.

The room went pitch black.

He felt bad for the men and women still in the plant and for the workers who had just arrived for the day shift, people he'd worked with for over a decade. They wouldn't be returning to their families either.

By now the plant's internal emergency phone lines would be severed, leaving his friends to rely on their cell phones, if they worked at all, to communicate with their loved ones for the last time. Most would suffer thermal and radiation burns and then quickly perish from the lethal dose of radiation.

Tears filled Umar's eyes at the thought of what would be coming next.

For a split second, survival instinct kicked in, and he wanted to run. But running wouldn't save him. Nothing would. At least he'd be at peace, knowing his family was safe, vacationing on a Caribbean island far away from California—away from the fallout.

The floor below his feet shimmied then shook violently. The steel control room door blew outward, taking out half of the outer wall. Chunks of cement, wood, metal, wiring, and sections of control panels rained down around him.

The shock wave from the second blast catapulted him backwards and slammed him into the bottom of a cabinet next to the row of alarm panels. He felt the bone in his arm crack and shatter on impact.

Dazed and in agony, Umar lumbered to his feet. Dust and choking gray smoke filled the air. He yanked the collar of his shirt up over his mouth and nose, in hopes of shielding his lungs from the thick smoke.

It won't matter. It will be over soon.

It seemed as if a lifetime had passed before the third bomb rocked the facility.

If the explosion was successful, it would destroy the plant's main structure, setting off a massive catastrophic fire and taking out the emergency water feeding system used to cool the reactor's cores. Then, within minutes, one of the reactors would overheat and explode, sending a plume of radiation into the atmosphere, spreading deadly particles hundreds of miles across the United States, depending on the direction of the wind.

High-pitched emergency sirens wailed, alerting anyone within a ten-mile radius that something horrible had happened at the plant. Within minutes, the San Luis Obispo County warning system that extended from Cayucos in the north to Nipomo in the south would begin to howl.

The intense heat melted patches of skin on his face and bare arms, the pain unbearable. Umar's throat and lungs burned, and he prayed it would be over soon.

He dropped to his knees and wheezed for a breath, scarcely able to whisper his last dying words. "Allahu Akbar."

Then he slowly raised his head and stared into the eye of the raging fire roaring toward him.

CHAPTER TWO

Barstow, California - Five days later…

Hal Decker stared through the night vision binoculars trained on the living room window of a non-descript two-story house across the street. "Donahue, she's got a kid. Looks like a girl about five—six years old." He lowered the binoculars.

"That information wasn't in any of the background or recent intel we have on her. Maybe the kid isn't hers? Perhaps she's babysitting?" Angela shifted in the van's driver's seat and she grabbed the thermal imaging camera from the dash and turned it on. The device beeped to life.

"I doubt a rogue CIA operative is freelancing as a sitter. Would make a pretty good cover, though. Besides, the interaction between her and the kid screams mother and daughter. Lots of smiling, hugging and kissing."

"We're clear. There aren't any other heat signatures inside. Just her and the child. Looks like they're heading upstairs now. So how do you want to do this?"

Hal glanced at his watch. Seven-forty-five. "Very carefully. She'll kill us first then ask questions. If we spook her at all, she'll be on the run again. She's not the easiest person to locate, especially when she doesn't want to be found, which is one hundred percent of the time. We got lucky finding her in our neck of the woods. Last I'd heard, she was in Nebraska or something."

An upstairs light turned on. Then he witnessed the woman pull the curtains closed. She was probably getting the child ready for bed. "You had better contact Chambers and let him know about the kid. See what he wants us to do. He's going to have to figure it out because we can't take a kid with us."

Angela nodded. She pulled her cell phone out of her jacket pocket and made the call.

Trent Chambers wasn't going to be happy about the news. His old boss at the Bureau was an asshole on a good day, and considering they'd all experienced the worst day ever, Hal predicted Chambers was going to be a royally pissed-off asshole when he learned about the kid, especially when he wasn't aware of her existence. The guy didn't like complications, and this was definitely a wrinkle in the plan.

A few minutes later, Angela ended the call and shoved the phone back into her pocket. "That was a blast."

Hal grinned. "I bet."

"I can see why you left the Bureau. The guy's got quite an attitude." She lit a cigarette and unrolled the van window enough to let the smoke out. "He said go ahead as planned and to use the child as leverage if the woman doesn't agree. He'll have someone here to pick up the child in a half-hour and take her to a secure location until this is over. He also said wait until the other agents arrive. They'll be here in twenty minutes."

"That doesn't leave us much time to do what we need to do."

Fat raindrops splattered against the windshield and thunder rumbled in the distance. His gut twisted. He didn't like the idea of taking the kid away from her mother and using her as a pawn. That's not the way Hal worked. But things were different now. They didn't have a choice, especially now with a new threat, one that could cause another meltdown at another nuclear facility.

They needed the best, and Raina Storm was exactly that. She was a highly-skilled former CIA agent, what some called a 'covert specialist', a fancy name for an assassin. She was an expert in martial arts, weapons, and a dozen other things that Hal wasn't sure he wanted to know about. The woman was the last person on earth you would ever want coming for you because you'd never see her until it was too late.

Over the years, Hal had heard a lot of rumors about Storm, that she'd retired, gone off the grid, but never believed much of what he had heard. Most people thought she was just a figment of some agent's over-active imagination. At least, that's what many FBI and CIA agents believed too. They were all wrong, including himself. Raina Storm was real. A legend. A lethal one.

Hal glanced across the street at the house. The light in the living room was still on, now partially obscured by blinds. Every few minutes, he noticed a tall shadow move back and forth in front of the window as if someone was pacing. "Are you going to be okay doing this if we have to use the kid?"

Angela flicked her cigarette butt out the window and leaned her head back on the headrest. "We have to. We need Raina. She's spent a lot of time in Central and South America. A lot of time. More than you and I have. Chambers is right. There is no other way. If we have to use the child, then that's what we have to do."

He looked at Angela, her short black hair glistening under the streetlights. They'd met during a mission in Colombia after Hal's good friend's fiancée, Whitney Steel had been kidnapped by Pablo Sanchez, once the top leader of the *Sur del Calle* cartel, Colombia's largest drug trafficking organization. Angela had been their lucky ticket home, risking her life to get them out of the country safely and back home. She was ex-military intelligence and a freelancer just like him, called upon to aid in sensitive covert missions—missions that usually involved national security. In this case, they were part of the taskforce team who were going to hunt down the terrorist cell responsible for the nuclear plant attack and who was threatening to do it again at another undisclosed US nuclear facility.

The aftermath of the attack at the Diablo Canyon plant sat heavy in Hal's mind and heart. Seventeen-hundred people had died, mainly workers arriving for the day shift, and many more were left with severe burns and radiation poisoning. They weren't expected to live. Hal imagined the death toll would skyrocket over the coming days, weeks, and months.

Right now, he and Angela were parked in a sparsely populated area on the outskirts of Barstow, California, about two-hundred-and-seventy miles northwest of ground zero. Hal wondered about the nuclear fallout that had blanketed a fifty-mile radius surrounding the plant. How far had the radiation traveled inland? There wasn't much that scared him, but radiation sure as hell did. He had a feeling what the terrorists had planned next would be deadlier, possibly killing tens of thousands and putting hundreds of thousands of people at risk of long-term radiation poisoning. Not to mention the devastating effects on the environment, animal life, and the food and water supply. Exactly why the terrorist cell needed to be found and stopped before the next attack. Enough damage had already been done. Enough lives lost. He noticed the light in the living room turn off.

Angela twisted in the seat and glanced over her shoulder. "Looks like we've got company. Doesn't look like the type of vehicle Chambers would send."

Hal checked the rear-view mirror as the set of headlights slowly rolled to a stop behind them. "It doesn't. Chambers wouldn't send a pickup truck to transport the kid. That much I do know."

The dark silver Ford 250XL parked, and the driver shut off the engine. A few minutes passed before the driver and a passenger exited the truck.

"These guys don't look right. They look too wired. I have a bad feeling about this." Angela grabbed her weapon from under the seat.

"Me, too. We don't need another complication." He watched through the tinted window as the two men dressed in black windbreakers and jeans hurried across the street.

The driver reached behind his back into the waistband of his jeans and pulled out a gun. He continued up the sidewalk and stopped in front of Raina's house while his passenger jogged around the corner of the structure, clearly heading to the back of the house.

Hal snatched up his Glock 17 on the seat next to him. "Shit. We need to take care of this."

Angela nodded, then got out of the van first and kept her weapon hidden in her coat pocket.

Hal opened the door and climbed out. He eyed the driver standing at the front door of the house trying, to peek in the living room window. "Take the back. Be careful."

"You, too." She shoved her hands into her coat pockets and walked briskly up the street, looking as if she belonged in the neighborhood then disappeared around the corner of the home.

A dog barked in the distance. A horn honked.

Hal raced across the street. The cold night air bit at his face and made his eyes water. He crouched and inched along the tall bushes out of the man's view.

Glass shattered.

Hal crept up the three cement stairs, keeping his Glock aimed at the back of the driver's head just as the man reached his hand through the door's broken pane of glass, ready to unlock it. He pressed the barrel of the gun against the back of the man's skull. "Put your hands up where I can see them, asshole."

The man froze and slowly raised his hands.

Hal grasped the gun from the man's hand and tucked it in his jacket pocket. Then he seized the guy by the back of the neck and shoved him up hard against the brick next to the living room window. "Who are you, and what are you doing at this house?"

"I'm looking for a friend of mine," the driver said.

Hal caught a slight British accent when the man spoke. "Right. I always go to a friend's house with a gun in my hand. Makes sense to me." He spun the man around. "What's your friend's name?"

The man glared at him and smirked.

"Yeah. Just what I thought." Out of the corner of his eye, Hal spotted Angela walking beside the passenger with a big grin on her face. He knew that look. She'd probably just kicked the guy's ass.

After Hal secured the driver, he and Angela escorted the pair to the van. "Chambers can deal with these two clowns. No clue who they are. They aren't carrying any IDs."

"Considering they're both wearing Kevlar vests and their weapons have suppressors, I think it's safe to assume this was supposed to be a kill."

"Agreed. But they weren't counting on us being here." Hal looked at the men sitting on the curb and then across the street at the house. *She has to know we're out here.*

"Glad we were. I don't want to think about what could have happened." Angela leaned in and kept her voice low. "Don't worry about Raina. She isn't going anywhere. I disabled the vehicle behind the house after I incapacitated driver-guy."

"Good. Keep your eyes on them for a couple minutes. I'm going to check their truck." As he walked away, two black Buick sedans pulled up. Hal waved at the agents as they parked the vehicles.

After Hal finished searching the truck, he heard the passenger yelling. The two had already caused enough trouble. He figured Raina was either watching the commotion, or she was upstairs, packing up the kid, preparing to take off. Either way, their plan of surprise had gone south, thanks to two unknowns looking to take her out.

"Keep that bitch away from me! She kicked me in the balls!"

Hal marched down the sidewalk and grabbed the passenger by the back of his shirt. He yanked him up and held him in the air, leaving his feet dangling before he lowered him and gave him a shove. "Shut the hell up, or she'll kick you again." He looked at one of the four agents that had just arrived and gave the man a push in their direction. "He's all yours. At least the other one knows to keep his mouth shut. There's also two AK-47s and a Beretta 92F in the pickup. Tell Chambers we need to know who these jokers are as soon as possible. Let the others know we should have our transport ready in thirty."

While the agents secured the men in the back of one of the vehicles, Angela and Hal got back into the van to get warm and figure out their next move.

Angela lit a cigarette and took a long drag. "What's the plan now? Our element of surprise just got flushed down the toilet." She took another drag and blew the smoke out the window. "It's not as if we can just knock. Raina isn't going to answer the door and welcome us in. After what just happened, and with her daughter inside, she'll kill us. She might be a top operative, but she's also a mother who will do anything to protect her daughter, especially if she feels threatened. That makes her even more dangerous."

Hal agreed. A woman protecting her child would do anything, including kill without so much as a blink. He checked his watch one last time. Eight-forty.

"We're going to have to take our chances. Too many lives depend on us getting her and now. The window's closing quick if we want to stop the latest terrorist threat. The whole operation rests in Raina's hands. She just doesn't know it yet." He rubbed his chin. "We already have an entry point thanks to one of the jokers. We'll go in through the front door. Let's just hope she doesn't kill us before we have the chance to convince her why we need her."

✳✳✳

Raina stood in the darkness and watched through the corner of the living room blinds. She had no idea who any of the players were out front but imagined they were probably connected to someone she had pissed off or killed or both.

Their bags had been packed for the past four months, ready to throw into the car, a precaution she had in place since she'd moved to Barstow, in case they needed to make a quick escape. This looked like one of those times. She stared at the pile of broken glass from the front door, glistening under the yellowish light coming from the streetlights, and then back outside.

Someone had found her, and she needed to get Jayden out of here, to somewhere safe. She hurried down the dark hallway and through the kitchen to the back door. With a pistol clutched in one hand and car keys in the other, she slid back the heavy metal bolt lock then turned the secondary lock. Raina cracked the door open a few inches and scanned the yard and trees shadowing the property to make sure no one was waiting for her. She exhaled a sigh of relief when she didn't spot anyone. Confident it was safe, she grabbed the two suitcases from the floor and crept down the six steps on the deck to the driveway.

Raina tossed the bags in the trunk and closed the lid, then ran up the deck's stairs three at a time and back into the house to gather Jayden from the upstairs bedroom. When she reached the hallway, hairs on the back of her neck stood up, and her legs froze.

Something caught her eye to the right— movement in the far corner of the living room, like a blur of fabric.

She crept catlike along the length of the dining room wall and two-handed the Walther PPK, a weapon she'd removed from the last target she'd been forced to kill before coming to Barstow. Her eyes roamed the darkness for any other signs of someone inside. She didn't have a chance to register the soft footsteps approaching from behind until an arm looped around her throat, and she caught the faint scent of floral perfume and freshly washed hair. Female or male, it really didn't matter. Raina rammed her elbow into the intruder's ribs. The woman grunted and released her neck then stumbled backwards into the wall with a thump.

Raina's pulse thudded in her ears. She spun and gripped the weapon at eye level, searching the darkness. She couldn't see the woman, but by the sound of boot heels scraping against the floor, she surmised the woman was scurrying down the hallway toward the front of the house.

The living room light flicked on.

"Don't even try it," a male voice said.

Raina stared at the towering man with hard blue eyes and blond hair clipped high and tight—marine style. He was big, maybe six-two, maybe two-hundred and thirty pounds and all muscle. The barrel of his Glock was aimed at her heart. Her gaze shifted to the stairs then back to the man. *Jayden.*

"Put the gun on the floor. Now," the woman ordered.

She smiled at the tall and slender woman who appeared to be around the same age as her with short, black cropped hair tucked behind her ears.

"Do it, or so help me God, I'll blow your knee out, and you won't be walking around with your child for quite some time," the woman said.

She knows about Jayden.

Panic built in Raina's chest and the walls closed in around her. Bending slowly, she placed her weapon on the floor and forced herself to remain calm.

The man toed the handle of the gun out of the way and sent it spinning like a top across the hardwood, out of her reach. "Get flat on your stomach and put your hands behind your back."

She did as instructed. With the side of her face splayed against the floor, all Raina could think about was her daughter upstairs. Her gut told her they were safe because if the intruders had wanted them dead, they would have been by now. She saw the female's brown boots step toward her and felt her hands being secured roughly with double ties. Arms looped her elbows, and she was quickly dragged to her feet.

"We just want to talk to you," the man said.

"You could have asked nicely."

His eyes narrowed, and he kept his gun directed at her chest. "And if I had? Would you have made it easy for us?"

He had a point. Not likely. "Undo my hands right this minute."

The man shook his head. "Sorry. Not happening."

"Please, I need to check on my daughter." He looked to the woman who had finished unbuttoning her coat and was rubbing her left side.

"Angela, can you check on her?"

"Sure."

Raina watched the woman leave the living room and heard the stairs creak with each heavy step. "Are you going to tell me what's going on?"

"My name is Hal Decker. That's Angela Donahue. We work for the US government."

"CIA?"

"No."

"Please undo me."

"No."

"You're a man of few words."

"So I'm told. Anyway. I assume you heard about the terrorist attack at the Diablo Canyon nuclear plant last week?"

"Who hasn't? What does that have to do with me?"

Angela strutted back into the room with Raina's purse and dumped the contents into a pile on the couch. "Your daughter is fine. She's sound asleep."

Raina breathed a silent sigh of relief.

"After the attack, under the direction of the president, a covert terrorism task force was formed, mainly made up of CIA, FBI, and ex-military. Angela and I are part of the team whose mission, codenamed Operation Oblivion is to hunt down the terrorist cell."

She wasn't happy about where the conversation might be going. "Again. What does any of this have to do with me?"

"The terrorist cell is threatening a second attack at another nuclear plant. At this point, we don't know which one. According to a CIA agent on the ground, the terrorists have a large dirty bomb they plan on transporting into the country via Colombia and then up through the Mexican-US border. We have a small window to stop them before they reach the US. Less than a week."

Angela held up Raina's driver's license. "Oh. Look at you, Clara Addison." She tossed the ID on the couch. "Nice name. Pretty generic. Too bad it's not yours."

She glared at the woman. "What do you want from me?"

Angela grinned. "You're now part of our team."

No. She wasn't. She couldn't leave Jayden. She wouldn't. "The hell I am. I have my daughter to look after."

Hal took two steps and stopped, his weapon still pointed at her. "That's exactly why you are going to help us. Because you love your daughter. If there's another attack, it will kill thousands, perhaps hundreds of thousands. No one is safe. Not you. Not your daughter. For all we know, the cell could be targeting the Yucca Mountain Nuclear Waste Repository. That's not very far from here, is it?"

Raina had to get Jayden out of the US, far way. Somewhere safe. Maybe Bangkok.

"We need your help. We can't do this alone. You've spent a lot of time in Central and South America. You know the terrain and the people. You have connections," Hal said.

She wasn't going to do this. Her daughter came first, and now that Raina was aware of a second attack—no way. "I can't help you. Now untie my hands and get out of my house."

Lines etched his forehead. "We figured you would say that."

"Hal, do you want me to wake up the child and get her ready for transport? "Angela asked.

She glared at Angela again. "You're not taking my daughter anywhere."

"Since you won't help us, you've given us no choice. Let me tell you what's going to happen next. Jayden will be taken into custody right now. Afterwards, she will be sent to a foster home. Do you really want your daughter in the foster care system like you were? How did that work out for you?"

Raina's eyes narrowed, and she wanted to snap the woman's neck. "You bitch."

Angela sat on the arm of the sofa, and her expression softened. "Look, Raina. We're not here to hurt you or your daughter but believe me, we *will* do whatever it takes to make sure you agree to help us. You have options here. If you agree, you have Hal's and my word that your daughter will be looked after and will be safe until the mission is completed. After that, you're free to do whatever you want—leave California for all we care. Helping us sounds like a much better option to me than having Jayden tossed around in the foster care system. It's your choice."

A tense silence filled the room.

Raina forced the images of her father, a nasty drunk, and how she'd killed him in self-defense when she was sixteen, back into the deep recesses of her mind where they needed to stay locked away. She didn't like the fact that Angela knew so much about her. As soon as they stopped the terrorists, Raina would take Jayden and disappear again.

"Besides, those two guys we stopped from killing you tonight said others would be coming. I have no idea who you pissed off. Don't really care," Hal said. "But lady, your daughter isn't safe here. She'll be safe in the FBI's custody. I promise you that."

More than anything she wanted Jayden to be safe. She didn't have a choice. She thought about everything that could go wrong, including the possibility of the dirty bomb exploding while they tried to stop the terrorists. If something happened to Raina, who would care for her daughter? Silence answered her. She needed to have a plan in place. "Okay. I'll help. On one condition."

Hal slowly lowered his weapon. "What's that?"

"If something happens to me during the mission, promise me you will keep Jayden out of foster care— that a loving family will be found immediately for her through private adoption only. I want this set up through a lawyer before we leave. That's the only way I will do this."

He glanced at Angela then back to Raina. "That's not an unreasonable request, considering the danger involved with this operation. We can have the papers drawn up first thing in the morning. Again, you have my word."

He seemed genuine and she believed the man. Raina nodded. "Now will you please remove the cuffs?"

Hal stared at her for a long moment as if contemplating if he should or not. Under different circumstances, he'd be a fool to release her because she wouldn't think twice about killing him. He tucked his gun in his pocket.

Angela reached behind Raina's back and removed the zip-ties then picked up the Walther PPK and set it on the coffee table.

Raina rubbed her red wrists. "Now what?"

"We have two agents ready to take Jayden to a secure location, a safe house, a couple hours from here in Las Vegas."

Raina wasn't keen about Jayden leaving, but it was the right thing to do. Whoever those two men were earlier, more would come. She wasn't going to put her daughter's life in jeopardy again. "Can I see the place?"

"Yes. We'll stay there until morning. That way you'll be able to spend some quality time with your daughter before we leave."

At least she would be able to check out the place and know Jayden was safe. "Our suitcases are already packed in the trunk of the car out back."

"I'll put them in the transport vehicle," Angela said as she headed toward the kitchen.

Raina heard the familiar jingle of the car keys she'd dropped in the hallway when Angela had tried to stop her.

Hal leaned against the wall and crossed his arms over his chest. "Any idea who sent those men, and why they're after you?"

It was sort of a silly question, considering her line of work. It could be anyone. One thing she'd learned, it could sometimes take months before her past caught up with her. Just when she started feeling safe, the past would rear its ugly head and, in most cases, force her to leave a trail of bodies in its wake.

Raina gathered her wallet, driver's license, gun, and tossed them into her purse. "Apparently, someone who isn't too happy with me."

"You got that right. We'll see if we can get an ID on your two friends." He paused for a second. "Are you ready to go?"

Raina nodded. "I'll go get Jayden."

"I'll take the purse and bring your daughter down for you." Hal held out his hand.

She hesitated then handed him the shoulder bag. "You don't trust me, do you?"

"Just playing it safe. You're an assassin. I'd be an idiot to trust you completely."

She shook her head. "You had better start trusting me, otherwise, this mission is doomed."

CHAPTER THREE

Raina was nothing like Hal had imagined or expected. Her green eyes told a story, one of sacrifice, death, and survival. It was hard to believe the woman was once the CIA's deadliest operative. At five-foot-ten and a hundred and twenty-five pounds of sculptured muscle, she was drop dead beautiful in a natural way. Absolutely stunning and utterly deadly. Jayden had the same long brown hair as her mother. No doubt about it. The kid was damn cute. Hal wasn't sure how old Raina was but figured about thirty and had already lived a lifetime three times her age.

Two hours and fifteen minutes after leaving Barstow, Hal watched the taillights of the sedan ahead transporting Raina and Jayden turn right onto Tropicano Avenue. At nine-thirty, the temperature outside had dipped to forty-five degrees Fahrenheit. Snowflakes danced in the air and evaporated instantly on the windshield. It was cold and wet. Not the typical Las Vegas weather most tourist-types envisioned.

"She's right, Donahue. We have to trust her if this operation is to succeed," Hal said.

Angela turned the heat on and flicked the wipers on low. "After she almost busted a couple of my ribs with that elbow shot, I think I'll stick to a little distrust for a bit longer. At least until she proves herself."

Hal checked the van's side mirror and spotted the same black Jeep Cherokee following them since they left California. After the incident at the house, he wasn't feeling too comfortable with a vehicle trailing them, and his gut was telling him the same thing.

Angela adjusted the rear-view mirror and unrolled the window a few inches. "You seem on edge. Worried about who's behind us?"

"He's been following us since about three miles outside of Barstow. I'd rather be safe than sorry." He grabbed his cell phone and called the agents ahead in the sedan.

"Yeah."

"Robson. Tell Russler to take a detour down a couple of the side streets. We might have a friend tagging along for the ride. Hopefully, I'm wrong."

"You got it."

The transport vehicle's brake lights flickered, and the car slowed then turned onto Harrison Drive.

Hal straightened in the seat and watched in the side mirror as the driver of the Cherokee followed Angela's lead. He glanced over his shoulder and continued to watch. The Cherokee suddenly stopped in the middle of the road.

Two cars swerved around the vehicle. Horns blared.

Angela gripped the steering wheel with two hands. "What is he doing?"

"I don't know. Maybe he knows he's been made."

Seconds passed, and the driver gunned the engine and did a U-turn. Tires squealed. Then the driver sped back in the opposite lane toward Tropicano Avenue.

"Okay, that was a little weird even by Las Vegas standards." Angela lit a cigarette and took a drag.

He didn't like it one bit. "It's too weird for me." Hal called Robson again. "Be on the lookout for a black Jeep Cherokee with rental plates. If you spot the vehicle anywhere near the safe house, keep going and meet us in the parking lot at the coffee shop on Flamingo."

"I'll let Russler know. Our ETA is about six minutes."

Hal ended the call and balanced the cell phone on his knee, his eyes scanning every side street and driveway as they passed, expecting to see the Cherokee again. But he didn't. "This is supposed to be the easy part, getting the kid to the safe house. The hard part begins tomorrow." He paused for a moment. "You know you can still change your mind about the mission. I'd understand and so would everyone else involved."

Angela glanced at him then back at the road. "You know I don't have a significant other and I don't have any children. Honestly, I'd rather be doing something than sitting around wondering if the world was going to end because of another nuclear disaster. I signed on to help make a difference, and I'm following this through to the end. Besides, you really do need me to protect you from Raina. I guess you're stuck with me."

Hal laughed. He was glad he was stuck with her. He had liked Angela from the moment they'd met in Colombia. They'd tried the dating thing, but after a few weeks, decided they were better at being friends than lovers. He also knew he could trust her—that she would always have his back.

The transport vehicle turned onto Harmon and continued east. When they neared the end of the street, Hal spotted the US Marshals' black SUV parked two houses away from the safe house.

Angela wheeled the van in behind the sedan and parked underneath a streetlight. She shut off the engine and grabbed Raina's purse from between the seats.

Hal got out first and looked up and down the street. Not a soul in sight. Shadows danced in unison across the sidewalk from the overhanging trees lining the road. The neighborhood was quiet. Always had been. He remembered when he was still with the Bureau. Many of the agents hated the location, citing the area was 'too suburban' with too many backyards where someone could hide. But the safe house was one of the most secure and state-of-the-art facilities the Bureau owned.

Russler and Robson exited the transport vehicle at the same time while Raina lifted Jayden out of the car. The kid opened her eyes for a second then her heavy eyelids closed, and she drifted back to sleep with the side of her face resting on her mother's shoulder.

"Let's take them in through the back in case we have some nosy neighbors," Hal said to Robson as Russler opened the trunk and collected the suitcases.

As they walked together to the safe house, the hair on Hal's arms stood up. He grabbed his gun from his jacket pocket and held out his arm signaling for everyone to stop.

The windows in the Marshals' SUV were splattered with blood and brain tissue. Shattered safety glass sat in a pile on the curb, decimated from a gunshot blast. Russler and Angela readied their weapons and inched cautiously on either side of the vehicle.

Angela peeked inside the driver's window. She looked up at Hal and shook her head.

"They're both dead," Russler said. "Gunshot wounds to the head."

Hal couldn't believe it. Matt Thompson and Terry Price were good guys. Trusted guys, men with families, who'd been with the Marshal Service for over twenty years. He shook the thought from his mind and focused on the mess they were in.

Raina clutched Jayden and crouched next to the tree beside Hal. "You said we'd be safe. You gave me your word."

She was right. They should have been safe. The location had been comprised, and Hal was running out of options. Moving to a hotel was out of the question. Too many security issues and no time to put the proper measures in place, and he couldn't move Raina and Jayden to the safe house three hours away in Warm Springs because it was occupied. At least if they stayed here they could employ the state-of-art security features, plus he'd make sure Chambers beefed up security, locking down the area if need be. Hal would do whatever he had to. No one was getting in that house.

Angela was on her knees beside Raina and slung the purse off her shoulder, letting it drop at her feet. "Russler and I will get your daughter inside. She'll be safer in the house than out here on the street. We don't know what or who we're dealing with."

Raina looked at Angela for a long moment then finally passed Jayden to her, who was still asleep. "If anything happens to her, you know I will kill you."

Angela held the kid tight. "I wouldn't expect anything less from you." She turned to Russler. "Let's go. We'll call Chambers once we're inside."

Hal watched them creep along the bushes and up the neighbor's driveway next to the safe house. Less than a second after they were out of sight, a bullet whistled past his head. Another shot drilled into the corner of the front bumper of the SUV with a hollow thump.

"I can't see where the shots are coming from," Robson said as he two-handed his gun.

Hal's eyes roamed the street and the shadows. "I don't see anyone."

A high-pitched whine bit the night air, sounding much like a small, low-flying plane.

"What the hell is that?" Robson scrunched down lower, unsure where the sound was coming from.

Hal wasn't sure either until he spotted a bright red remote-control car speeding toward the SUV with a square package duct taped to the top of it.

A bomb.

The radio-controlled car halted under the bumper of the SUV.

The whining stopped.

"Get out of here!" He turned and grabbed for Raina's arm, but she was gone. "Shit."

Hal and Robson bolted a half block in the opposite direction and dove for cover behind a wooden fence.

The explosive device detonated.

The force of the blast lifted the front tires of the SUV off the ground and slammed the vehicle back down on the street with a loud bang. Glass shattered, and chunks of bumper scattered into the street. Smoke mingled with the cold night air as orange flames engulfed the vehicle and raced up the tree, devouring the branches and leaves within minutes.

***

Raina squatted in the bushes across the street. Male voices reached her, and she counted two men dressed in black. She didn't want to kill them unless necessary because she needed to know who they were and who had sent them. Worry tore at her insides, and she prayed Jayden was safe with Angela and Russler.

One of the men, the taller of the two, was about two-hundred yards away, leaning against the hood of a black Jeep Cherokee with a transmitter in his hand. He placed another radio-controlled car rigged with explosives on the street. The engine roared to life and the toy took off. Suddenly, it stopped dead in the middle of the road. The man thumbed the controls, trying to get the vehicle working again. Another man stood directly across from him with a rifle aimed toward Hal and Robson.

Hal yelled at the half-dozen neighbors now congregating outside of their homes, watching the commotion, to get back inside and lock their doors.

Raina raised her pistol and fired. The shot took out the nearest streetlight, making it more difficult for her adversaries to see her coming. Shards of glass rained down and mixed with the light snowfall.

The man with the rifle fired blindly in the wrong direction, confused as to where her shot had come from.

She squinted in the darkness, and raced up a driveway onto a front porch, then climbed up on the railing and leapt over an overgrown hedge into the next yard. As she barreled through more bushes, sharp evergreen branches scraped her hands. Moving from shadow to shadow, Raina circled behind the Cherokee and crouched in the wet grass behind a tree.

A quarter moon carved through a litter of clouds for a brief moment and provided enough of a soft glow for her to see the man with the rifle walking down the street toward the safe house. The other man with the transmitter cursed in Arabic and threw the controller on the ground, clearly agitated that the second delivery device wasn't working properly.

Concerned there might be other men in the area she hadn't seen, Raina crept up behind the man. When she was close enough, she delivered a low, spinning sweep kick. The man's legs disappeared beneath him and he toppled hard onto his back knocking the air from his lungs. His head bounced off the pavement once, and he moaned. Stunned by the blow, he stared up at her with wide eyes and gasped for a breath.

Raina pocketed her gun and snatched her scarf from around her neck. With three quick movements the cloth was wound tightly around his wrists and the first threat was secured. She grabbed his keys and quickly searched the Cherokee. Inside, she found a roll of duct tape and a nylon rope, along with another rifle and two handguns. After ripping off a length of tape with her teeth, she plastered the tape over the man's mouth.

"When I get back, you and I are going to have a little talk."

Dragging the dazed man to his feet, she pushed him ahead to the light post. Once she had him tied to the base with the rope, Raina sprinted across the street, weaving in and out of the yards then long-jumped over a rock garden, searching for the man with the rifle.

Twigs snapped.

Raina reached for her gun.

She two-handed the weapon and edged along a garage with her back flat against the wall. Her eyes strained in the darkness. She thought she heard footsteps on the sidewalk. She dropped to the ground and aimed the weapon toward the street. Boots came into view, and rifle-man walked past her, unaware she was almost on him. He stopped at the wooden fence where Hal and Robson were hiding. He raised the rifle and took a step.

She wasn't going to allow the man to kill Hal and Robson.

A gunshot cracked.

The bullet ripped through the man's shoulder and spun him around.

She fired again.

The slug drove into the center of his forehead and sent him plummeting to the ground into a heap, next to the smoldering Marshals' SUV.

Sirens wailed in the distance and grew closer.

She climbed to her feet and brushed the dirt and grass from her hands.

Hal and Robson walked out from around the other side of the fence with their guns drawn.

Raina glanced at the dead man, and then at Hal. "Trust me now?"

CHAPTER FOUR

While FBI agents and the local cops rolled out yellow crime scene tape and secured the perimeter, firemen doused the metal shell of the burned-out SUV.

Hal stared at the man tied to the lamppost with nylon rope. "Any clue who he is?"

Raina shook her head. "But I'm going to find out." She ripped the tape off the man's mouth. "Who are you? Who sent you?"

The man ignored her and looked away.

Hal grabbed the man's face and jerked his head toward him. "She's talking to you. Deal with her or deal with me. I'm not that nice. Right now, you're looking at a death sentence for murdering two US Marshals. Maybe if you cooperate they'll let you hang out in prison for the rest of your life instead."

The man remained silent and continued to stare blankly past Raina.

"This isn't getting us anywhere. He's not going to talk. The locals are searching the rental. Maybe they'll discover more about him."

"I heard him talking in Arabic." Raina snatched the man's arm roughly and rolled up his sleeve. Then she checked the other arm.

Hal raised an eyebrow. "What are you doing?"

"Looking for tattoos. Many of the individuals and groups I've dealt with are usually inked." She bent his head down and spotted the black tattoo at the base of his neck. Afterward, she flung his head, making sure it smacked against the lamppost with a hollow thump. "SoA. Soldier of Allah. SoA is used on many jihadist web sites. Just like SWT is used by Muslims as an acronym for *Subhanahu Wa Ta'ala*, Glory to God."

Hal rubbed his chin. "Then you know who sent him and why?"

"I think I know who might have sent him. Followers of a Muslim imam by the name of Aasif Abu Shakra. He recruited mainly out of Yemen, using the Internet to call on all Muslims to wage a war against the US and other countries." She paused for a moment then continued. "He's not so charismatic anymore, though. He's dead. A knife was plunged into his heart six months ago."

"By you?"

She paused for a moment. "Yes."

Why didn't that surprise him? Hal wanted to know who had paid for Shakra's death but decided the less he knew, the better. "From what I remember, he was also a senior recruiter for al Qaeda."

"He was." The wind picked up, and Raina stuffed her hands in her leather jacket pockets. "So is his brother, Abdul."

Hal didn't like where the conversation was going. Was the attack at the Diablo Canyon Nuclear Plant and the assassination of a high ranking al Qaeda recruiter connected? Raina knew exactly what he was thinking by the somber expression on her face.

He waved to one of the agents to look after the guy tethered to the post then turned to Raina. "Come on. You look like you're frozen. I need to call Chambers to find out who was working at the nuclear facility on the day of the attack and see if anyone was associated with Aasif Shakra or his brother."

***

While Hal was on the phone, Raina checked on Jayden sleeping in one of the three safe house bedrooms. Even after what had happened earlier, she was confident her daughter would be safe here. The front door of the fire-proof, two-story home contained steel plates and a fully bolstered steel frame. All the windows were fitted with one-and-a-half-inch bulletproof Plexiglass. Not necessarily fail-proof, but it would create some stopping power long enough to buy some time to get Jayden to safety.

From what Hal had told her earlier, the FBI had also purchased the two bungalows on either side of the house years ago. They were currently rented to employees at the Bureau. The added security gave her some much-needed comfort, knowing there were extra agents right next door.

She had already noticed the satellite dish on the roof, used for backup communications. There was no way anyone could get into the house undetected. Between the state-of-the-art security system providing real-time information on intruder sounds and locations, concealed interior and exterior motion sensors and cameras, it would take an army to bust in, and by then Robson and Russler would have her daughter secure in the metal-encased panic room, waiting for backup.

She sat on the edge of the double bed next to Jayden and stroked her chubby cheeks. The last thing she wanted to do was to leave her daughter. Raina didn't have a choice. Not now.

The attack on the nuclear plant was probably payback for something she had done—for killing Aasif Shakra. Little did anyone know it was a high-ranking official with the Syrian government who'd paid to have the man assassinated. She couldn't change what had already happened, but she could try to make things better. The only way to do that was to locate the al Qaeda terrorist cell and ensure the dirty bomb never reached the US.

Raina pulled the blanket up around Jayden's chest and gently kissed her forehead then stood and peered out the window at the continuous flashing blue and red lights. She'd never seen so many agents and cops in one spot before. FBI, Las Vegas cops, state troopers, US Marshals, and the medical examiner. Usually, she was the one running away from scenes like this. Instead, she was right in the middle of it. At least now, she knew who she was up against. Shakra and his clan played for keeps.

After closing the bedroom door, she headed down the hallway to the open concept kitchen lined with glossy white cupboards and stainless-steel appliances.

Angela shut the laptop lid and looked up when she walked into the room. "Is she still asleep?"

"Yes." Raina grabbed a bottle of water out of the fridge then pulled out a chair and sat at the round glass table. "I'm surprised, considering all the commotion out front." She eyed the wall clock. It was twelve-thirty in the morning, and she had a feeling it would still be a couple more hours before she could get some rest. She opened the bottle and took a drink. "Tell me what you know about the dirty bomb."

Angela leaned back in the chair. "Eight months ago, nearly 55kgs of uranium stored for scientific research disappeared from a university in northern Iraq. On the same day, four-hundred-and-twenty-million dollars was removed from Mosul's central bank."

"Former al Qaeda territory. Now re-branded under ISIS, the al Qaeda's splinter group. That's quite a bit of money." Raina said. "More than enough to plan and pay for another attack on US soil."

"Exactly. It will definitely grease a lot of palms along the way. According to one of our assets, a CIA agent on the ground, a large bomb was built and transported by container ship from Yemen to Venezuela four days ago. From there, it was moved by truck into Colombia where it's being protected by the *Sur del Calle* cartel."

The thought of a dirty bomb in a country with dozens of militant groups scared the hell out of Raina. Anyone of the groups could steal the bomb and do whatever they liked with it. She tried not to think about it. "Why is the cartel involved? On one hand, you have a terrorist network made up of fighters linked to the Islamic State of Iraq and Syria, and on the other, you have the cartel who deals in drugs and guns. I don't understand the connection."

Hal walked into the room with a can of beer in his hand. He leaned against the granite counter. "For starters, money, and revenge. After Pablo Sanchez was killed, his number-one-in-command, Alejandro Quintero, started running the show. Quintero vowed he'd seek revenge for Pablo's death, for the man who was like a son to him."

"How do you know this? Last I heard, Quintero was with the Colombian National Army."

"He hasn't been for a few years." He took a long gulp of his beer and set the empty can beside him.

"How are they planning on getting the bomb from Colombia to the US? There's a lot of miles in between. By ship?"

Hal looked at Angela then back to Raina. "We heard by land, up through Central America and then into Mexico, but to be honest, we don't know for sure. That's why it's important for us to stop them while they are still in Colombia. You asked what the connection was between the terrorist cell and the cartel—Alejandro Quintero knows how to move enormous amounts of drugs and weapons undetected into numerous countries including the United States. He's been doing it for over three decades and has never been caught. When Pablo was alive, Quintero was head of the cartel's US network. If anyone can get a bomb into the states, Quintero can."

A terrorist cell partnering with the *Sur del Calle* drug cartel. The perfect marriage. Now, it was beginning to make sense, and Raina didn't like what she heard. The mission was even more dangerous then she first thought and much deadlier than what she was told. "We take out the terrorist cell and then what? What about the bomb? We can't leave it there. Imagine what FARC or the ELN or one of the other radical groups would do with a bomb if they got their hands on it."

There was a long pause of silence before Hal spoke again. "We blow it up."

"You want to blow up a dirty bomb that produces a blast wave of radioactive material in the middle of drug cartel country." She laughed. "Are you two crazy?" This was a death mission. They'd be lucky if they made it out alive.

Hal pulled out a chair and took a seat. "Look. I never said this operation was going to be easy and didn't come with some major risks. I can't guarantee we'll make it back but think of the alternative if we don't do this. Think about your daughter and about what happened at Diablo Canyon Nuclear Plant less than a week ago. There were one-hundred-and-forty public schools and thirteen hospitals within the fifty-mile contamination zone. We have to shut down this new threat entirely otherwise Diablo Canyon will happen again, just somewhere else. It's the only way."

Raina remained silent and thought about what Hal said. She had done a lot of things that could be classified as crazy during her time with the CIA and afterwards. She'd taken part in operations around the globe but detonating a radioactive bomb would be a first for her. There had to be another way. "What about dumping the device in the ocean?"

Angela shook her head. "Too risky. You know Colombia better than anyone. You know the dangers, and it's not just the checkpoints everywhere. The cartel, gangs, guerillas, militants, and the list goes on. There's no way we can safely haul a bomb cross-country to the ocean without risking getting shot at. One bullet and kaboom. At least, this way, we're in control. We blow it up like Hal said. Then we get the hell out of town." She pushed out her chair and stood. "I'm going outside for a smoke."

After Angela left the room, Raina's thoughts drifted to Jayden and the life she finally had with her daughter. She was just starting to get to know the little girl after she had been kidnapped by her ex-husband, Daniel Martínez, son of a Colombian diplomat she'd met during one of her many operations in Colombia. With the help of another CIA agent who'd gone underground, off the radar decades ago, they were able to get her daughter safely out of Colombia and back to the United States.

A hard knot formed in her stomach. She was terrified that Daniel would come to take Jayden away again, but this time Raina would be ready for him. And she would kill him. If it wasn't for the CIA agent's help, Jayden would still be with her ex-husband. Her daughter was only two years old when it happened, too young to remember why her mother suddenly disappeared from her life. It was a time Raina didn't like to think about or talk about, the pain of losing her child still too raw. She had just gotten Jayden home less than six months ago. Their new mother daughter future had just begun, and if this mission went south, their life together would be cut short. Way too short.

"Want a beer?" Hal opened the refrigerator and pulled out two cans.

"Sure."

He slid one across the table to her.

She cracked open the can and took a drink. "Do you have a location of the bomb?"

He spun the laptop around and within a few seconds the screen filled with a map of Colombia.

"According to the last intel we received two days ago, it's here in the jungle on the outskirts of Pablo Sanchez's old compound. The area is infested with cocaine labs and booby-traps."

"Great. One of those labs could blow and so does the bomb. You're full of good news."

The more she learned, the more Raina didn't want to go, but she knew she had to.

"Any ideas on how we can get into the country undetected? Last time I flew directly into La Florida Airport posing as a businessman. Not sure I want to try it again without a contact on the inside."

"Maybe." She'd have to find someone she could trust. "What about weapons?"

"We've got that covered. There's a Colombian *casa de seguridad* here in Tumaco." He pointed to the map. "It was used by a friend of mine, a police captain with the National Police. The safe house even has an underground bunker with weapons, ammunition and electronic equipment that was confiscated from the cartel and militant groups."

At least they didn't have to worry about gun power. But they had another problem. Raina was running low on people she could trust and couldn't think of anyone they could use off the top of her head. She didn't want to ask her CIA agent friend. He had already done enough. "Can your police friend get us into the country?"

Hal shook his head. "He was killed during the last mission I was involved in." He looked away and stared toward the hallway. "Believe me, if Oscar was alive, he'd be the first to help. He was a good guy. One of the few cops who wasn't tarnished by the cartel's money and power."

She detected the sadness in his voice. It was the same way Raina felt about leaving Jayden, a muddled mixture of melancholy and fear at the thought of possibly not coming back to her. She had to remain focused. Get this operation done. Then come home to her daughter.

"Hey. Look what I found. Cheese and pepperoni and deluxe." Angela grinned and balanced two large pizza boxes in one hand and her package of cigarettes in the other." Russler and Robson are in the living room. They already scooped over half of one of them." She set the boxes in the middle of the table then opened a cupboard and passed a stack of paper plates and napkins to Hal.

After they had finished eating. Raina pushed her plate aside and snatched another bottle of water from the fridge. She was full and tired and needed time with her daughter. "I'm going to try to get some sleep."

"Try to come up with someone who can get us into Colombia. In the meantime, Angela will work her magic on getting us out. That's her speciality. Exit plans. The paperwork from the lawyer, regarding Jayden will be here for you to sign by eight in the morning. She'll be fine with the guys. Robson has two four-year-old girls. Twins."

That didn't make her feel any better. She headed down the hallway to the bedroom, dread flooding through her again. She could kill without so much as a blink, using poison, knives, a piano wire to strangle, her hands, a bullet, or explosives no larger than a throat lozenge to blow apart a target's head, but she was about to fall apart at the thought of leaving her daughter with a stranger. She inhaled a deep breath and fought back the tears.

After changing into an army green tank top and gray sweat pants, she crawled into bed next to Jayden and watched the gentle rise of her daughter's chest. She looked so peaceful, almost angelic beneath the glow from the streetlight. Raina lay there, her eyelids heavy, and listened to the muffled voices filtering in from outside, hoping things would quiet down soon. The thought of another attack on a nuclear plant scared her to death. She wanted to pack up Jayden and run far away from here, far away from anyone or anything that could hurt her daughter.

As she drifted off to sleep, the last thing she remembered was Jayden's sweet face and then Raina was in the middle of the Colombian jungle, running for her life.

❋❋❋

"I was right. Chambers confirmed the attack at the nuclear plant is probably linked to Raina. The explosive device attached to the remote-control cars were pipe bombs rigged with C-4, the identical setup Assif Shakra had used to kill a US diplomat in Yemen two years ago. The bombmaker's signatures matched. I'm pretty sure Raina already knows the terrorist attack and what happened here tonight are connected."

Angela frowned as she cleared the table of the empty pizza boxes and paper plates. "That's a huge burden for someone to carry around. A lot of people died and are still dying."

"Chambers said a man by the name of Umar Sarouk had been a nuclear engineer at the plant for over ten years. When his home was searched, they found a note to his wife and children. He made it clear his alliance was to al Queda and to Aasif and Abdul Shakra, his childhood friends."

"Now we know who and why. But I'll ever understand how anyone can terrorize and kill innocent people. How the hell did Sarouk get a high-level security clearance to work at a nuclear facility, to begin with? His connection alone to the Shakra brothers would set off a huge red-flag."

"I don't know. Either someone screwed up or looked the other way. I'm guessing by the way these guys work, someone was forced to look away, more than likely threatened.

"Sarouk was a sleeper. He'd been waiting years to be called upon to fulfill his duty. His chance to step up to the plate and support his friends presented itself after Raina killed Aasif." Hal stood and set the empty beer cans on the counter. "From the evidence gathered so far, it appears the attack had been in the planning stage for the past seven months. I was going to tell Raina everything, but I think she's got enough on her mind. She's apprehensive about leaving her daughter. Who could blame her? It can't be easy."

"I doubt it's easy. She's doing the right thing by helping us. A lot of lives will be saved if we can pull this off."

Hal nodded. "I gave Russler and Robson the heads-up to be on the lookout, in case she decides to bolt with the kid. I don't think she will. I'd rather be prepared if she decides to, though. Chambers also has four extra agents covering the front and back of the house."

"I really don't think it would matter how many of us are here. Hal, if Raina wants to leave, she'll make it happen and take us all out if need be. She wouldn't think twice. She's a cold-blooded killer. That's what makes her the best."

"I know. Believe me, I'll be sleeping with one eye open. I suggest you do, too."

CHAPTER FIVE

After a restless night and a quick cold shower, Raina signed the legal documents stating that if something happened to her, Jayden would be privately adopted and never placed in the foster system. She took a sip of her coffee and watched her daughter sitting at the kitchen table with a coloring book and stack of crayons.

"Momma, I'm hungry."

"Yes, baby. I'm getting your breakfast."

The little girl held out a crayon and her eyes twinkled. "Red."

"That's right. Your favorite color." Raina finished slicing a banana and wiped her hands on the dishtowel.

Jayden grinned then lowered her head and continued to scribble, using long bold strokes, the expression on her round face intense, the way she squinted, and her eyebrows came together.

Raina placed a Styrofoam plate with bananas and four squares of toast smothered with peanut butter beside her.

Jayden's eyes lit up. She dropped her crayon and shoved the coloring book across the table.

Her heart squeezed as she watched her daughter eat breakfast. God, she had to make it back. She had to. Jayden needed her as much as Raina needed her daughter. Her eyes shifted to the clock. In twenty minutes, she would have to leave with Hal and Angela. A hard knot formed in her stomach and she tried to ease down the panic bubbling inside. "Momma has to go to work soon."

The little girl looked up at her with wide eyes. "Don't go." She popped a slice of banana into her mouth.

Guilt filled Raina's soul at the thought of leaving, and her hands trembled. She was about to lie and tell her daughter that she'd be home in a few hours, but she couldn't do it. Normally, she could. Kids at this age really had no sense of time. This time was different because the truth was she might not come home at all. Raina turned and poured another cup of coffee to shield Jayden from seeing the tears filling her eyes for the second time.

"Done, Momma."

Raina inhaled a steady deep breath then exhaled, determined to calm her nerves. When she was ready, she turned to find Jayden with her head cocked to one side, holding out her empty paper plate, proof she'd finished her breakfast.

"You're such a good girl."

As if sensing something was wrong, Jayden suddenly frowned.

Raina forced a smile to reassure her everything was fine. "Momma loves you very much. You're going to have fun today."

Her daughter loudly smacked her lips against the palm of her hand and blew Raina two kisses and giggled.

Her heart melted. It was exactly what she needed. She wanted to remember Jayden happy. At the moment, she was.

Then time stopped, and so did her happiness when Hal poked his head in the kitchen and mouthed. "We need to get going."

✳✳✳

Raina stared out the window of the plane. Lakes and rivers transformed into splashes of blue paint against the multi-shades of lush green tree tops resembling bunches of broccoli—her daughter's favorite vegetable.

The last image imprinted in her mind as she walked out the front door of the safe house and drove to McCarran Airport was that of her daughter sitting cross-legged on the living room floor, trying to toss Cheerios into Agent Robson's mouth. Each time Jayden missed and hit his nose, she burst into laughter and clapped her hands with glee.

Now, seven hours after leaving Las Vegas, Raina, Hal and Angela were about to land at Tocumen International Airport in Panama. From there, they'd catch a flight to a small airstrip in Jaque, a small coastal town filled with refugees from the Colombian town of Juradó pushed into Panama when the Colombian civil war ended.

Angela sat across from her in the aisle seat, thumbing through a fashion magazine and sipping a cocktail. Raina had to admit the woman looked strikingly beautiful with her eyes heavily lined in black and muted shades of green and brown shadow that made her eyes pop against her shiny black hair.

Hal sat in the seat beside Raina and downed the rest of his Heineken. "Are you sure you can trust your man, Alfaro?"

Raina hoped so. She had called Serigo Alfaro first thing this morning, and he didn't sound too impressed to hear from her. She was confident his attitude would change once he received a large payment for his help.

He was a rodent-looking man, an underground contact specializing in fake IDs for the now-defunct Nino's Ricos gang in the Panamanian port of Colon. The last time she had used his services, he'd tried to rip her off, demanding an extra ten-thousand-dollars for identification she desperately needed. He learned quickly not to mess with her after she rammed a seven-inch blade into his thigh, reminding him she wasn't happy about his untimely and unfair price boost.

She leaned her head against Hal's shoulder and kept her voice low, so the passengers seated behind them couldn't hear her. "Serigo knows if he double-crosses us, I will come for him personally. So, yes. We can trust him, but once we're in Colombia, we're on our own. It's not going to be easy."

"I know it's not. We'll figure it out."

Out of the corner of her eye, she noticed Angela looking at her strangely. Then her eyes narrowed.

Raina held her gaze and realized the woman didn't like how close she was to Hal. She had seen that death stare many times during various missions over the years. She looked away as the plane's landing gear touched the tarmac and the seat belt tightened around her abdomen.

Angela appeared to be jealous. Not a good thing, since they all needed to work together and trust each other for the operation to succeed. There was no room for error or failure. Raina hoped the jealousy thing wasn't going to be a problem because she was tired and cranky due to a lack of sleep and the two-hour time difference. Right now, she really didn't feel like kicking Angela's ass to keep in her in line.

By the time they'd exited the plane and cleared a complete security check, it was eight-thirty at night and they were all hungry. After visiting the food court on the second floor and discovering the main restaurant was closed, they settled on a hot dog from one of the many vendor carts. At least the fast food would tide them over until they landed in Jaque.

Although the airport was clean and airy and had large windows overlooking the tarmac, there was an underlining feeling of apprehension she couldn't shake. Her eyes roamed the security lines, boarding gates, and car rental desk area, not sure what she was looking for—maybe a face or a gesture that didn't fit.

Hal finished the last bite of his hot dog and wiped his mouth with a crumpled paper napkin.

Angela touched her arm. "Is something wrong?"

"I'm just tired. It was a long flight. I think I'll take a walk and check out the tax-free shops before we catch our next flight. Want to come with me?"

"Sure. I need to stretch my legs." Angela grabbed her handbag from the chair beside her and looked at Hal. "Back in a bit."

He glanced at his watch. "Make it quick. We need to board in twenty minutes."

Raina brushed her bangs out of her eyes and slung her black leather bag over her shoulder. This was the perfect opportunity to talk to the woman and see what was up with the death stare earlier.

As the two strolled through the airport, Raina surveyed each person's face. The feeling something was off was stronger than ever. The sooner they boarded the flight to Jaque, the better. A dark-skinned man in his mid-thirties with the face of a wrinkled dog looked her up and down unable to keep his leer to himself. He seemed out of place, dressed in an expensive black suit, compared to the colorful attire of the tourists trickling through the spacious airport.

Raina stopped inside a cosmetic shop and pretended to check out the different shades of pink lipstick. "You have nothing to worry about when it comes to Hal. He's not my type, Angela."

The woman laughed and shook her head slowly. "I don't know what you're talking about. From here on out, let's stay focused on the operation, okay? I think we have enough to worry about—like staying alive."

"Agreed." The hairs on her arms stood up. Raina casually picked up a compact and opened the round case. She used the mirror, angling it enough to see who was behind her.

The dog-faced man peered in the shop window.

She had an excellent memory, and this guy didn't look like someone from her past. Not to say she hadn't met him somewhere, like in a dark alley in Panama or beneath the streets of Bogotá.

She snapped the compact closed and whispered to Angela. "We need to go. I think we're being followed."

Angela didn't turn around. Instead, she followed her lead and left through the other door of the shop.

As they walked past the window, Raina eyed the man behind them.

"A friend of yours?" Angela asked.

"No." Raina wanted to stop and ask him why he was tailing them but didn't want to direct any unwelcome attention to the situation.

All they needed to do was board their flight without any issues.

Ahead, she spotted Hal with their tickets in his hand. He waved.

Her heels clicked with each step on the shiny floor, and heavy footsteps closed in behind her.

"You dropped this," a male voice said.

Raina spun and stared at the man. She was positive she'd never seen him before. She would have remembered that face.

He shoved a folded piece of paper at her then scurried past Angela and disappeared around the corner and out of sight.

Worry electrified the air.

Hal raised an eyebrow, his voice full of concern. "What was that all about? Know that guy?"

She had no clue who the guy was. Raina unfolded the paper and read the message scrolled in barely legible handwriting.

Hotel Chavala - Jaque
Room #32 under the name Mrs. Alfaro
Serigo

Raina's stomach tightened. Her contact always demanded that they conduct business on his own turf, usually at his shop outside of Yaviza. She passed the paper to Hal and wondered if their lives were in danger before they even got to Colombia because Serigo would never set up a meeting in a hotel unless he felt threatened.

CHAPTER SIX

After an hour-long flight, which was as bumpy as their landing at the small airstrip in Jaque, Hal was able to find a cab to drive them to Hotel Chavala.

The four-storey, L-shaped hotel was nothing special, bland and old, located in the center of town. The outdated lobby was decorated in red and gold. Oil paintings of fishing boats and wildlife hanging on the walls looked like they might have been painted by some of the area's indigenous people. Three large ceiling fans with straight wooden blades churned a steady, swirling breeze of hot and humid air throughout the lobby. Hal cursed under his breath and wiped the sweat from his forehead with the back of his hand. He hoped, at the very least, the place had air conditioning in the rooms.

Hal and Angela stood by the elevator and waited for Raina to register at the check-in desk. Angela leaned against the wall and flipped through a two-day-old copy of *El Siglo*, a Spanish language newspaper. The terrorists had chosen the perfect venue to get the world's attention. Nothing like an attack on a nuclear facility to make everyone take notice. Even after almost a week, the pages were cluttered with images of the aftermath at Diablo Canyon Nuclear Plant.

The bold headline on the front page read, "*Otro Chernobyl?*"

Another Chernobyl. This time it wasn't an accident.

The first picture showed how the vegetation surrounding the plant had absorbed much of the heavily radioactive dust, turning trees and plants to a vibrant shade of scarlet, like someone had dropped a huge bucket of paint over the area. Another photograph depicted an empty playground next to an abandoned school with backpacks and books scattered on the ground by children and parents who had rushed out of the area to safety. The last image, photographed in black and white, showed a sizable employee parking lot at the plant transformed into a vehicle graveyard filled with irradiated fire trucks, ambulances, and even a few helicopters used in the disaster. The images left a hollow pit in Hal's stomach, and he could tell they affected Angela even more by the way her eyes were glossed over.

"Things are never going to be the same again. In a way, we've lost a bit more of our freedom. Just like we did after 9/11." She slapped the newspaper closed and folded it in half.

He wrapped his arm around her shoulder. "You're right. That's the whole idea of a terror attack, to make people fearful and question their security. Umar Sarouk accomplished what he set out to do, kill and terrorize." Hal prayed the cowardly bastard had gone straight to hell where he belonged. "We can't allow the terrorists to strike again. We can't allow them to win."

She smiled and leaned her head on his forearm for a long moment then straightened when she spotted Raina walking toward them with a room key in her hand.

Raina snatched the handle of her suitcase. "Come on."

They walked down a long hallway and then veered to the right before stopping in front of the blood-orange painted door with a small silver plaque marked with the number thirty-two. Light spilled out from under the door across the scratched and worn tile floor. Twenty yards away, Hal noticed a small exit sign at the end of the corridor, grateful they were on the main floor if they needed to depart in a hurry.

Raina exhaled a deep breath and eased the key in the lock and turned. She glanced at Angela and then to Hal. Gripping the handle, she slowly turned the knob and opened the door.

"You're here. I was beginning to worry," a man said.

The first thing Hal noticed was the refreshing blast of cool air circulating in the room. He looked at the olive-skinned man with close-set eyes and long narrow face dressed in a blue tropical print shirt and beige cargo shorts. The shape of his face reminded Hal of a rat—long and pointed. "This must be your contact, Serigo Alfaro."

Raina nodded. "This is Hal. That's Angela." She dropped her suitcase at her feet. "Why are we meeting here, Serigo, and not at your shop?"

Angela went and checked the bathroom and then the large closet in the hall, making sure no one else was in the room. "All clear."

"Oh, it's nothing really," Serigo said. "I had a little trouble with a former gang member. Nothing I can't handle. I thought it would be better for us to meet here. I figured you'd be pleased I'm looking out for your safety. You know you can trust me."

Hal doubted she needed anyone to look out for her. She'd proved that back at the safe house. He could tell by her narrowed eyes, she wasn't buying the man's story. There was more to the brief explanation than he was telling her.

"What did you do, Serigo? Try to rip off the gang member like you tried with me?" Raina opened the bar fridge, grabbed three bottles of water, and handed one to Angela and Hal. "Remember what happened with the knife?"

The man looked away. "Of course, I remember. I still limp sometimes because of it."

Raina gulped down a quarter of the bottle of water and set it on the table. "Sometimes people need a lifelong reminder for their past poor choices, especially if they think they can cross me. I'm sure it won't happen again."

The man fiddled with his fingers and sweat beaded his forehead. "It—won't."

"Okay. Let's get on with why we're here." Hal looked at the Panamanian, determined to find out how this rat-looking man was going to get them to their destination. "How do you plan on getting us into Colombia?"

Serigo reached into his pocket and pulled out a hand-drawn map. He passed it to Hal. "Everything is ready. A Picuda will meet you at the mouth of the Rio Jaque in an hour and a half. It should take you less than fifteen minutes to get there from here. One of my trusted associates will be waiting for you and will make sure you get into the country. I have also made arrangements for a vehicle for you."

Hal was aware of the Picuda boats used by the cartel to deliver and smuggle drugs into Costa Rica, Honduras, and Jamaica. A go-fast boat was their best option for traveling in the middle of the night and getting to their destination quickly. He also knew there were risks: rough seas, getting caught, and a guy who used the word 'trust' too many times. He was feeling uneasy about the last one.

"I bought the items you asked for, Raina." Serigo pointed to the shopping bags heaped on a chair. "The other supplies, the Hazmat suits, gloves, boots, respirator masks, and iodine tablets are on the boat. They were a bit more difficult for me to get my hands on. You'd be surprised what you can buy on the Panamanian black market." He paused for a second, looking as if he wanted to ask Raina what the items were for. Instead, he glanced at the door. "I should probably go and let you get organized."

Raina patted the man on the back and hustled him toward the door. "Thanks for the help. The money will be transferred into your bank account the moment we leave Panama. You never know, if all goes well, you might even receive a bonus. But if you've set us up—I'll come back and slit your throat."

***

After a short cold shower, Raina combed her hair back into a high ponytail and secured it with an elastic band. She pulled on a black tank top and her usual black cargo pants, an outfit that would allow her to move freely, but wasn't the best choice for the steamy tropical weather. When she was done, she found Hal and Angela sitting at the table.

Angela had changed into a loose-fitting short-sleeved top, black jeans and running shoes. Hal was dressed in two-tone brown army pants and a dark brown T-shirt. Angela had a concerned look on her face, and Hal didn't look much better.

Raina knew exactly what they were thinking about. Serigo.

"I'm concerned about your friend. Can we trust him?" Hal twisted and tossed an empty water bottle in the oval waste basket against the wall. "I didn't get that type of vibe from him—the trusting kind."

"He's scared. It's obvious he's angered someone who isn't going to let him forget it." Raina hoped that was all it was. She had no idea what the man had done. She could only guess it involved a large sum of cash, which explained why he didn't hesitate when she had asked for his assistance. Usually, he'd hemmed and hawed before agreeing to help her. Serigo didn't, this time. He jumped at the chance, making her question his motive even more.

Angela lit a cigarette and took a long drag. Rings of smoke hovered around her head, rose to the ceiling, and disappeared. "Doesn't it worry you that someone might have followed him here, putting the mission at risk, as well as our lives? If something happens to us and we don't destroy the bomb, the consequences will put your daughter's life at risk."

Raina cocked an eyebrow. As if she wasn't aware of that. It was the only reason she was here. The only reason she'd agreed to help, to make sure Jayden had the best chance at a happy and long life, even if it was without her mother. A heavy emptiness weighed on her chest like a lead brick. She missed her little girl more than she could ever say. She forced the thoughts to the back of her mind, determined to remain focused on the operation. The sooner they got to Colombia and found and detonated the bomb, the sooner she could go home and see her daughter.

She sat on the edge of the bed and put on a pair of running shoes then rested her elbows on her knees. "If he was followed, then we deal with it. We won't have a choice." She checked her watch. "We should get moving soon. Are the backpacks prepared with the supplies?"

"They're by the door. You just need to add the personal items you want to bring. Your friend also brought each of us a weapon. They'll come in handy until we get to the safe house in Tumaco," Hal said.

Raina stood and inspected the Beretta 92FS on the table. She always liked the weapon's short recoil, delayed blowback system, and the ability to chamber individual rounds in the event that magazines were lost. It happened sometimes when you were running for your life. She tucked the pistol into the waistband of her pants and snatched up the box containing fifty rounds of 9 mm ammo. Serigo had come through for them, but she questioned his nervous behavior and thin explanation as to why he chose to meet at a hotel, a crappy one at that.

She crossed the room and picked up her backpack. She opened her suitcase and tossed a change of clothing, some toiletries, her passport and wallet into the knapsack. When she was done, Raina slipped the straps over her shoulders while Angela tightened the narrow strips of cloth on hers.

"I spoke to Chambers while you were in the shower. Jayden is doing fine. She's having fun with Robson. I thought you'd want to know before we leave. Everything is okay," Hal said.

Knowing her daughter was happy and safe made her feel a bit better. "Thanks."

Minutes later, she locked the hotel room, and they walked down the hallway to the exit sign.

✳✳✳

Outside, the air was like a thick fog, stifling and humid. Stars sparkled like polished jewels as a half-moon lit their way through the deserted streets. According to the brochure in the hotel room, the fishing town didn't offer much, other than a small hospital, grocery store, a few other hotels, and a handful of places to eat. Certainly not your highly popular tourist destination.

They made their way through the dimly lit streets clogged with simple square houses painted in muted shades of yellows, blues, and reds. Across the street, a small brick police station was covered with green camouflage netting. A light shone in the front window.

Five houses up, they stopped and slipped around the corner of a house. An older model motorcycle crept by with its engine coughing and spitting. Raina watched the driver make a left, finally finding the right gear, and sped off.

She looked up and down the street and then at the map. "We're about a block and a half from the river. There's another police station, a bunker, located right at the mouth of the river. I'm hoping there will only be a skeleton crew working since it's the middle of the night. It's not as if the town is crime central. The most action cops around here see are from drug smugglers and human traffickers trying to sneak into Jaque by boat."

"We should probably go east one block, circle back, and hike along the river. The bank will provide us with a bit of cover," Angela said.

Hal swatted away a large winged bug trying to land on his forehead. "That's exactly what I was thinking. Put some distance between us and the police bunker until we spot the boat."

Ten minutes later, they reached the river. The bank was slippery and mucky and not the easiest to climb down, especially wearing rubber-soled running shoes. Tips of branches slashed Raina's bare arms, and mud sloshed under her shoes. She was relieved when her feet hit the level sandy beach. The humidity was heavy and overpowering, even though a light wind rolled off the ocean. While Hal and Angela stopped and shared a bottle of water, she looked across the river at the dozens of round huts with thatched roofs built on eight-foot wooden stilts situated at the edge of the river. Behind the structures stretched a thick jungle canopy as far as she could see.

"There are four indigenous villages within about twenty kilometers. The beaches usually aren't patrolled at this end," she said. "At least, they weren't the last time I was here."

"How long ago was that?" Hal stuffed the empty water bottle into his backpack and wiped the sweat from his forehead.

"About nine months."

"A lot can change in that amount of time. Keep your eyes open. We don't need any surprises. Stay close to the bank."

Branches snapped, followed by rustling sounds like someone walking on dried leaves.

Raina, Hal, and Angela spun with their weapons drawn at the exact same time.

Raina squinted in the moonlight and caught movement. She breathed a sigh of relief. No real sign of danger. A three-foot-long capybara rummaged along the undergrowth, grazing on grass and tree bark.

Angela lowered her gun. "The thing just about gave me a heart attack."

As the large rodent stripped off leaves from the bottom of a towering fern, it made clicking and chirping sounds then looked at Raina and purred. "They're pretty much harmless. Quite friendly."

Hal slid his gun back in the waistband of his pants. "Friendly or not, I'm not too keen on giant rats with heads the size of large dogs. The thing looks like it weighs a hundred pounds." He shook his head. "We need to keep moving."

As they trekked farther down the beach, the hum of a motor powering down grew louder.

Hal and Angela shrank into the shadows along the bank and out of sight. Raina crouched next to a tree, her gaze glued to the action a hundred yards away in front of the police bunker. At first, she thought the boat was their ride until she noticed it was a

Panamanian National Police boat. The driver docked the boat in front of the bunker and cut the engine. Another officer tossed a heavy rope around the front pole on the dock, looped it twice, and then performed the same action at the back pole. Two men in two-tone green camouflage uniforms complete with AK-47s and wearing Kevlar vests emerged from the watercraft and proceeded to stand on the dock, speaking to each other in Spanish. Both men lit cigarettes and continued talking, their voices drifting in and out of the wind.

Worry worked through her body. The men were going to be a problem, and there were probably more inside the bunker. She stood and glanced at her watch. Their ride would be arriving in less than ten minutes.

She stayed low and crept to where Angela and Hal were hiding. She waited and watched the dock area. "We need to take these guys out. Otherwise, we're not going to get out of here. We don't have much time. The boat will be here soon."

Hal glanced at Angela. "We'll take the two on the dock. Raina, you take the bunker."

Raina nodded. "Give me a minute to get inside."

She two-handed her weapon and scrambled along the edge of the bank, the heels of her shoes digging into the sand. Insects buzzed around her face and bit at her skin, and she swore she swallowed a dozen gnats. Weaving in and out of the shadows, she kept her eye on the two men on the dock and scurried up an incline. Raina stopped at the side of the bunker and ducked below the window. She inched her head up and peeked inside.

A man wearing shorts and a T-shirt lay on the floor with a gaping wound to the center of his chest. A stream of blood outlined his body and pooled beside him. Feet away, another man dressed in an officer uniform had his rifle aimed at Serigo.

What was going on? Why was Serigo here? Raina's pulse sped up, and she gripped the handle of the gun tighter. The only logical explanation—he'd set them up.

After wriggling the backpack off her body, she grabbed the straps. She should shoot the little weasel between the eyes for selling them out. She should never have trusted the man. She glanced over her shoulder and waved at Hal and Angela, signaling them to make their move on the men on the dock.

Loud tempestuous gunshots pierced the tangy air. Birds scattered in confusion high over the treetops. The two men dropped off the side of the dock simultaneously and into the water with a splash. Their bodies caught the current and floated down the mouth of the river and out to sea. Raina moved backward a few steps then jumped to her feet. She hurled the backpack through the window. Glass shattered and rained down onto the floor of the bunker. The man spun and pointed his weapon toward the window. Serigo tripped, his feet slipping beneath him as he skittered out the door.

She fired.

The bullet drilled through the center of the officer's forehead, thrashing his skull back and forth. His arms became animated, dancing like a marionette, then he fell to the floor against the wall. From the corner of her eye, she spotted Angela running down the beach after Serigo.

Raina sprinted across the sand, hoping to catch up with him, surprised how fast the man could run. She would never have pegged rodent-face as a track and field kind of guy, but he was running for his life—and he knew it.

Angela caught up with him and reached out, ready to grab the back of his shirt. She missed.

Raina picked up her speed, her strides long and precise. When she was close enough, she jumped and spun halfway in the air. The heel of her outstretched leg connected with Serigo's shoulder. The hit drove him hard into the murky river, face first.

Angela stopped to catch her breath. Her face shone with sweat. "Raina—you didn't have to. I—had him. This is your fault. We shouldn't have trusted him."

She was right. Trusting Serigo was a huge mistake, one Raina wouldn't make again. She bent and rested her hands on her knees, inhaling and exhaling, willing her pulse and breathing to slow to normal. "You didn't have him. That was the point. But we do now."

"I guess someone had better fish him out before he drowns, even though he deserves to." Hal ran into the brown water up to the knees, rolled the man over, and dragged him by his arms up on shore.

The man moaned. Then his eyes popped open.

Raina straightened and glared at him. "Get up. Now."

He lumbered to his feet and rubbed his shoulder. Serigo looked at her and backed up a few steps.

"Who's the dead guy in the bunker?"

"I don't know. He was in the bunker when I got here. Maybe the officer caught him trying to sneak into Jaque."

Rodent-face was wise to move away from her because she was debating her options, which included snapping his neck. She didn't care why he was here. Right now, all she wanted to know was one thing. "Where's our ride?"

He didn't answer.

"Last time, Serigo. Where is our ride?"

She wasn't impressed and wanted to shoot him between the eyes. She took a step, but Hal instinctively slid between her and the man.

Serigo stood there for a long moment, not making eye contact, as if trying to decide on what he was going to say. "I—can't get you the boat or the other things until you pay me seventy-fifty-thousand dollars more. I don't have a choice. I'm sorry."

She could tell by the tone of his voice he was sorry. That didn't make her feel any better. They were losing valuable time. The sun would rise soon, bringing a new day along with a shift of officers to man the bunker, their chance of getting into Colombia would be lost.

Angela shook her head. "This is nuts. We could take the police boat."

Raina had thought about it, but they needed the suits and his connection to get them into the country. They didn't have time to come up with a different plan.

"Then you won't have the Hazmat suits and iodine tablets. I don't want to know what you're doing, but I assume the items are very important to you." Serigo wrung his hands and lowered his head.

"Once I have the payment—you'll have everything you asked for."

"You double-crossed us. You double-crossed me. You know this isn't going to end well for you, Serigo."

His body trembled, and his eyes filled with tears. "Please. Forgive me. I'm sorry. He forced me to do this. I'm out of choices."

Hal looked at Raina, and then to Angela. "Is he crying?"

Angela shrugged. "Why are we wasting our time with this fool? We have a boat. The sun will be up in less than two hours. Let's just go." She turned to walk away.

Hal grabbed her arm and stopped her. "Not yet." He gave Serigo a shove. "Who made you do it?"

"The guy I owe money to, the gang member. If I don't have the gambling debt paid by noon he'll kill my niece. He already has Pilar and won't give her back until I pay him. Please. She's only seven years old. Just a baby."

Raina's heart sank. She thought about Jayden and what she would do to save her daughter if she found herself in the same position. She'd do anything, exactly what Serigo had done.

"We need to get out of here and into Colombia. I'll make some calls. You will get the money." Hal's eyes narrowed. "In the meantime, get your guy here now with the boat and our supplies. Otherwise, I'll kill you myself and make sure you die slowly, knowing you killed your niece."

✻✻✻

While Hal sat on the beach at the mouth of the river and ended his call to Trent Chambers, Serigo paced across the sand, talking on his cell phone.

Hal didn't trust the man and wasn't going to give him one cent until he produced the boat and supplies they needed. Chambers wasn't impressed either, after being woken up in the middle of the night. Luckily, the importance of the operation overrode the man's foul mood, and he agreed to the extra payment with a condition to ensure they got to their destination safely and on time—they had to take Serigo with them. Once they were in Colombia, they'd cut him loose.

He stood and glanced at Raina and Angela sitting behind him on one of the steps leading to the bunker, drinking water and each downing an energy bar. Concern gnawed at his gut by the women's seemingly strained relationship. Both were extremely competitive, and suddenly, they were testing each other. He needed them focused and on top of their game for the mission to be victorious.

Hal heard the whining growl of engines long before he spotted the thirty-eight-foot blue Picuda slowly motoring down the dark river. Water churned and rippled ahead of the long and narrow fiberglass nose as the driver masterfully maneuvered the craft to the dock and powered down the engines.

Hal grasped his backpack and headed toward the bunker. Raina and Angela met him.

Serigo walked toward him at the same time. When he was two feet away, he stopped. "Did you get the money?"

"It will be deposited soon." Hal didn't want to tell the man, at least not yet, about the condition until he made sure the items they needed were on board, in particular, the much-needed Hazmat suits and respirators. "I want to see the supplies."

"Everything is there, the suits—."

"Considering what's already happened, I think we'd rather see for ourselves."

After Angela confirmed the items were in the boat, Serigo introduced their captain, a twenty-something dark-skinned man with thick, black hair and a well-trimmed goatee.

"This is Felipe. I've known him and his family for years. He can be trusted."

The man gave them a nod and remained quiet.

Hal wasn't feeling too comfy again with that word 'trust'.

It was time for Serigo to realize who was in control. And it wasn't him. "You're coming with us. Once we're in the country, then you can come back here and deal with getting your niece back. You have my word the money will be deposited in your bank account the moment we're in Colombia."

"What?" Serigo shook his head. "No. That wasn't the deal."

Raina reached for her gun. "I don't think you're in any position to negotiate. Those are our terms or no money."

The man looked at Raina with wide eyes filled with panic, and then back to Hal.

Taking the man with them was assurance he wouldn't be causing any more problems. Of course, Hal wanted the guy to get his niece back, but enough with the games. They didn't have time to waste. "Or Raina can kill you right now. Your choice."

Serigo's expression tightened. He glared at Hal, clearly not happy with the arrangement. "Fine. I'll go."

Minutes later, Felipe sped the Picuda along the Panamanian coast a half-mile from shore. The go-fast boat glided over the waves, cutting through the water with precision and stealth. The three two-hundred horsepower motors would get them to Colombia in half the time and made it difficult for radar to detect the all fiberglass body, making it the cartel's boat of choice for moving large amounts of drugs in very little time.

Moonlight reflected and cast a shimming glow across the water, lighting the way for a family of bottlenose dolphins breaching the bow waves coming from the boat. Hal was sitting next to Serigo, who looked terrified with his fingers dug into the sides of the seat. Raina and Angela were behind them in the back-to-back lounge seats, enjoying the constant mist of cool water spraying off the side of the boat. Hal was grateful for the temporary break from the humidity and happy they were finally on their way to Colombia. The sun would be up in less than an hour. Nothing else could go wrong.

After a half-hour ride, Hal spotted lights in the distance and the cranes at the Port of Tumaco working through the night, lifting metal containers off the ships and transferring them into the terminals. They were getting close. Felipe downshifted the boat, made a hard left and steered the craft toward the shore.

It was obvious their captain had made this same trip multiple times, probably running drugs for the cartel. The man slowed the Picuda about a quarter mile from the port and stopped the boat on a sandy reef hidden by the dense jungle canopy. He shut off the engines and hopped out. After securing the boat to a tree with the heavy line so it wouldn't drift away, Felipe helped unload the supplies.

Raina and Angela exited the boat with their backpacks and each grabbed a large box.

When Hal stepped out of the boat, a wall of hot humid air hit him, his body still vibrating from the ride. He picked up the last box and turned to Serigo. "How far from here?"

"The cartel has a path cut through the vegetation. We follow the trail for about ten minutes to the top where there's a vehicle waiting for you. We have to hurry. Felipe and I need to get back to Panama before daylight."

Hal wasn't too happy about going through the jungle with so little light. He remembered the last time he was in Colombia, how the cartel had boobytraps set everywhere to protect their coke labs, not to mention the snakes and jaguars. He tried not to think about the dangers and continued to follow Serigo. The guy had better be on the up-and-up this time because he if wasn't, Raina would kill him, and Hal wouldn't stop her.

As they hiked up the steep incline, small birds chirped, and branches swished overhead. At times, it was difficult to know where the noises were coming from. Sweat dripped off his forehead and stung his eyes.

When they finally reached a clearing with a makeshift dirt road, Serigo dropped the box at his feet then reached in his pocket and pulled out a set of keys. He tossed them to Raina. "My job is done."

Hal looked at the late model beige four-door Renault 16 TS. The perfect vehicle to use to fit into the Colombian landscape. He set his box down and watched Raina get into the car and start the engine. Seconds later, she popped the trunk and shut off the car.

She climbed out of the vehicle with a smile on her face. "Tank's full."

The car worked and was gassed up. Hal had had visions of Serigo double-crossing them again. He breathed a sigh of relief that they'd made it. While Felipe loaded the supplies into the trunk, Hal nodded to Angela to make the call to Chambers to transfer the money to Serigo's bank account.

Serigo logged into his online banking using his cell phone and paced anxiously, waiting to get the money.

"It shouldn't take too long and then you can get out of here." Hal dug a bottle of water out of his backpack and downed the liquid in two gulps.

While they waited for the transfer to happen, the sky grew brighter, preparing to ignite a new day. Serigo and his friend were cutting it close. They'd be lucky if they made it back to Panama in time.

Serigo held up his phone as if he'd won a gold medal. "The money's in my account." He looked at Hal. "Thank you." Then he turned to Raina and shoved his hands in his pockets. "I really am sorry. I hope you understand. My back was against the wall."

She nodded. "Consider the money as a bonus for getting us here. Now, go back to Panama and get your niece. I hope she's okay."

After Serigo and Filpe headed back to the Picuda, everyone loaded into the car. As Hal steered out of the clearing and turned onto the main road the first orange-hued rays of sunrise veined out across the horizon.

CHAPTER SEVEN

Hal steered the Renault through the busy stone-paved back streets of Tumaco, the poorest and most violent town in southwestern Colombia, where lines blurred as to who were bystanders, gang members, or part of the *Sur del Calle* drug cartel. Neglected and shabby brick and adobe houses lined both sides of the road. Motorcycles, the area's choice of transportation, painted in a rainbow of colors and in a multitude of sizes, weaved in and out of traffic. And Renaults. Lots of them.

Angela shifted in the passenger seat and leaned her head back on the headrest while Raina sat in the backseat taking in her surroundings. Both women were quieter than usual. They all needed rest and food.

Fifteen minutes passed, and Hal spotted the safe house ahead. He double-checked his rear-view mirror for the fortieth time making sure they weren't being followed. He slowed the car and steered down a long driveway shielded by tall wax palm trees waving in the ocean breeze. Stones crunched and spit out from under the tires.

He rolled to a stop and parked at the side of the white-painted wood-framed house with a cobalt blue tin roof and shut off the ignition. "This is it. Our home away from home for the next twenty-four hours or so."

"Doesn't look too bad. It's got to be better than the hotel in Jaque. That place was a dump," Angela said, as she and Raina got out of the car at the same time.

And much safer, Hal thought.

In the backyard, the earth was sandy, and the grass was slightly overgrown. Angela lit a cigarette and strolled to the end of the property, soaking up the early morning view overlooking Tumaco Bay. The baking sun glistened off the calm blue water. Sailboats mastered the wind while two large freight vessels were being escorted into the harbor. Hal had to admit the view was beautiful, compared to the dilapidated destitute section of town they had just passed through. He bent and wiggled one of the four square terra-cotta patio stones leading to the wooden tool shed and lifted it. Underneath, he found what he was looking for, the key to the safe house.

Raina pushed her hair out of her eyes and squinted in the sunlight. "Not a bad hiding spot."

"After Oscar was killed, his wife Mariana made sure there was always a key available in case the house was needed. Basically, an open invitation to everyone who was involved in the last mission."

"I thought this was an official police safe house," Raina said.

He shook his head. "The house belongs to Oscar and his wife. They've had it for about twenty years. It's only used by a couple of his trusted police buddies, a place they used to keep informants safe after they helped nail key players within the cartel. With over ninety percent of the Colombia National Police force on the cartel's payroll, it's hard to know who to trust, so not many know about the place. Which works in our favor."

Raina looked around. "It's far enough away from the road and secluded. The closest house is about a quarter mile away. It's a good spot."

As they walked to the front door of the house, Angela joined them and swung her backpack over her shoulder.

Raina looked at her and then at Hal. "Can I ask you something?"

"Sure."

"Were you the one who killed Pablo Sanchez? I'd heard an American had taken him out. I'm surprised it took so long for someone to get rid of him. The guy was a low-life murdering sonofabitch, killed tens of thousands of Colombians. I never had the pleasure of meeting him. If I had, I would have gladly put a bullet through his heart. Now we have to worry about Alejandro Quintero. It's still hard to believe the cartel is working with terrorists."

"They won't be for long. We'll make sure of it." He rubbed the stubble on his chin. "You asked about who killed Sanchez. A friend of mine, a former FBI agent. I was there when it all went down, though. Unfortunately, Oscar got hit during a shootout." Even though he trusted Raina, Hal didn't want to get into too many details, including naming names.

"I'm sorry about your friend."

Hal smiled and unlocked the door. "Thanks."

"What happened to his wife? Is she still in Colombia?"

"Last I heard, she was living off the grid somewhere. Not sure where."

Hal knew exactly where. Panama. She was staying at her sister's house in San Miguelito. No way would he ever put her life in danger by contacting her. She'd lost enough. More than anyone knew. Hal wasn't going to reveal that Oscar's daughter was living in the US with his friend, Blake Barnett and his wife, Whitney Steel. The fewer people who knew, the better. If the cartel ever learned that Oscar had played an instrumental role in Pablo's death they'd make sure Oscar's wife and daughter paid with their lives. An eye for an eye.

Hal wasn't going to see that happen. Just like he wasn't going to allow the terrorists to win.

The inside of the safe house looked the same as the last time he'd been here. Same chocolate brown couch and matching chair. The older model television, complete with knobs to change the channels and adjust the volume, sat on a dusty book shelf in the corner of the room. The house also had the same feeling of underlying danger, dark and foreboding, lurking in the stale air. The computer printer, digital camera, and other electronic equipment were still spread out on the desk constructed from two metal files cabinets at each end with a long plank of wood set on top, reminding Hal how the last mission ended. He flipped on the switch to the air conditioner. It chugged on, and within minutes, cool air began to circulate throughout the living room. It was weird being back here, where had Oscar died.

Hal pushed the thought from his mind and forced himself to remain focused and positive they'd all survive the mission. "Okay, ladies. We have a lot to do. It's going to be a long day and night."

Angela dropped her backpack on the couch and looked around the room while Raina was busy inspecting the windows and front door.

"Not bad. Solid steel front door. One-inch bars on the window." She tapped the glass. "One-and-a-half-inch bullet-resistant Plexiglass."

"At least we know we're safe in here. The moment we step outside, well, that's a whole different story," Angela said.

"You're right about that." He unzipped his backpack and pulled out a laptop computer. He set it on the desk next to the printer. "Wait until you see the bunker. You guys are going to be in heaven."

In the second bedroom, Hal bent and rolled up the oval area rug then pulled the bed away from the wall. He pressed his foot on the right corner of a three-foot section of worn linoleum. After he heard the click, the trap door sprang open.

Raina and Angela peered down the hole then looked up at him.

Hal grinned. "Ladies first."

Raina climbed down the rungs of the metal ladder first. Angela followed, and then Hal.

He ran his hand along the wall and found the light switch. He flicked it on.

Angela's mouth dropped open, her eyes lit. Then she grinned. "I'm impressed."

Raina echoed Angela's reaction. "Very impressive."

Open wooden crates overflowed with weapons from pistols to grenade launchers to drones and everything in between, as well as electronic equipment, including headsets, satellite phones, and GPS. Cases of ammunition were stacked on eight-foot-high heavy steel shelves, six rows deep. To the right, running the length of the house, were at least five years' worth of canned food and essential supplies stacked neatly on floor-to-ceiling shelves.

"All these weapons were confiscated from the cartel and militant groups?" Angela asked.

"Yeah. Oscar had been a cop for a lot of years. It might look like a lot, but nothing compared to what goes in and out of this country and is smuggled elsewhere."

While Angela inspected one of the three drones, Raina walked up and down each row, eyeballing the various weapons, probably making a mental list as to which ones she wanted to take with her.

It was ironic that the bunker looked like a fifties-style bomb shelter, considering their mission was to destroy a radioactive bomb.

Raina picked up a .300 Winchester Magnum, held it at eye level, and checked the scope. The sniper rifle looked huge against her small frame.

Fatigue and stress played havoc with every part of his body. Hal rubbed the back of his neck, his muscles tense and hard. "I'm going to check in with Chambers. Why don't you and Angela try to get a few hours of rest? I know we could all use some. Afterward, we'll get working on how we're going to pull off this operation without getting ourselves killed."

✳✳✳

Raina laid on one of the two single beds in the back bedroom with her eyes closed. She'd been tossing and turning for the past hour, unable to fall asleep. Apprehension about how Operation Oblivion would end plagued her thoughts. As happy as she was to see the stockpile of hardware and goodies in the bunker, reality hit hard. This mission could kill her. It could kill all of them.

She opened her eyes and thought about the cardboard boxes containing the respirators and Hazmat suits in the truck of the car. She had to have faith the gear would keep them safe. Hal had even requested a radiation detector which Serigo was able to surprisingly produce from one of his many associates in the black market.

Fear sent her heart rate soaring.

She wanted to fly home to Jayden and tell her how much she loved her. She missed her laughter and her smiling face. Her heart physically ached to have to be away from her. The child was her anchor and made her feel safe and loved, despite all the dangers in the world. Raina knew if she called her daughter, it would only upset the little girl. That was the last thing she wanted. She had to make sure she made it home alive. Their plan to blow up the bomb had to be solid. Rock solid. There would be no room for error.

Hal and Angela's muffled voices drifted into the room from the front of the house. Apparently, she wasn't the only one who couldn't sleep. She swung her legs over the side of the bed then padded down the hallway.

In the living room, Hal was sitting at the desk, working on his laptop, and Angela was scanning papers he'd just printed out. Maps of Tumaco and Bogotá were spread out across the coffee table.

Angela looked up at her and set the papers on her lap. "Doesn't look like any of us are going to get any rest."

"The anticipation of a mission always makes me a bit restless. This one even more so." Raina lied. She was more terrified that she'd die and not ever see her daughter again, a thought she decided to keep to herself and close to her heart.

Hal spun the chair around. "You won't believe what I found, Raina. Go take a look. It's on the kitchen table."

"There's also coffee in the pot," Angela added.

She hoped Hal was talking about fresh food, especially some fruit because she was hungry and wasn't looking forward to another chalky-tasting energy bar or cracking open one of the hundreds of cans of food in the bunker. Baked beans and tuna really didn't appeal to her this early in the morning.

The moment she walked into the eighties-style kitchen, she was dragged back in time. She glanced at the worn laminate countertops and then to the pink-and-purple-floral-printed wallpaper border surrounding the top of the walls and warm-hued wood cabinets. Raina poured a cup of coffee and then she spotted it on the kitchen table.

Excitement flooded her body. What she saw was much better than fruit, and instantly she knew exactly what Hal was thinking. Some of the anxiety she had felt earlier about the mission disappeared from her body and her muscles relaxed.

She sipped her coffee and gazed at the sleek black direct-fire weapon that the U.S. Army had hailed the 'game-changer'. The XM45 was the latest version of the XM25 first used in the war in Afghanistan. The XM45 Counter Defilade Target Engagement System was a high-tech rifle programmed to use advanced 25 mm ammunition. They'd be able to use the laser-guided weapon to detonate the bomb. Things were looking up.

"It has a range of about twenty-five-hundred feet, almost the length of nine football fields." Angela stood in the doorway clutching her coffee cup. "It'll allow us to put some distance between us and the bomb."

So, when the device exploded, they wouldn't be directly at ground zero. Raina set her mug on the table and picked up the weapon that might save all their lives, surprised by how light it felt in her hands, a little under fifteen pounds, she estimated. She had seen one before in Bangkok for sale on the black market, but she had never fired one. She doubted the engagement system would be difficult to use.

"There's a computer chip inside which communicates with the projectile calculating how far the round has to travel. It allows for precision detonation behind or ahead of a target. In this case, the dirty bomb."

Raina was surprised about how much the woman knew about the rifle, considering her expertise was more in the field of intelligence, surveillance, and reconnaissance. "How long does it take to deliver the round?"

Angela poured herself another coffee then leaned her back against the counter. "About five seconds. When the round is fired, it explodes with a blast comparable to two hand grenades."

The XM45 was exactly what they needed. The farther away from the explosion, the better. She set the weapon back in the case. The only problem now would be getting safely to where the cartel and terrorists were keeping the bomb. She'd been in Colombia at least a dozen times and knew that danger lurked everywhere. Her thoughts turned to Jayden again.

"Don't worry. We'll get you home to your daughter," Angela said.

"Am I that easy to read?"

"Not usually. You have a good poker face, except when you're thinking about Jayden. I can see it in your eyes, the love you have for her."

"Do you have any children?"

"Me? No. Thirty-three and single. I've always been a career kind of girl."

Raina knew exactly what the woman meant.

Angela set her coffee cup in the sink. "Hal wants to go over a few things about the mission. He said to be ready in about forty-five minutes, and I need to go work on our exit plan. You might want to grab a shower and an energy bar because it's going to be the longest day of our lives."

✳✳✳

By nine-fifteen they had finished eating canned chicken noodle soup and crackers. Not a filling meal, nor a typical breakfast, but they made do with what they had.

Hal looked at Angela and Raina, sitting across from him on the couch. "The latest intel that Chambers sent suggests Alejandro and the terrorist cell might be planning on moving the bomb early tomorrow morning by rail then loading the device onto a container ship. Destination: San Diego. If that's true, the cartel will use one of four ships at their disposal for smuggling drugs into the US. We need to destroy the bomb before they move it out of the area."

"Wouldn't it make more sense to detonate it when it arrives at the port?" Raina asked. "It would save us a long drive, and the area is more open and has lots of light around the terminals."

"If we blow it up at the port, it will kill a lot more people and destroy the ships in the harbor. Since we don't know what type of conventional explosives the terrorists have used with the device, I think it's safer if we blow it up in a more secluded area. Fewer casualties. If we go to where the bomb is, the only people in the immediate area are the members of the cartel, workers at the cocaine labs and the terrorists. There isn't anything around for miles where Sanchez's old compound is located."

Raina nodded. "Makes sense."

"Angela will look after the reconnaissance, so we can see exactly what type of enemy presence we're up against. We should probably take two drones, one as a backup, just in case we run into problems."

Hal passed Raina a printout. "I've calculated where you should be with the XM45. Here on the ridge." He pointed at the circle on the map. "It's about twenty-two-hundred-feet from the compound.

Getting there isn't going to be easy. This stretch of the jungle was rigged with booby-traps and there are a few of the cartel's larger cocaine labs." He leaned back in the chair. "As far as the actual compound is concerned, Sanchez used to have a tiger at the west end of the property secured in a cage. Since Alejandro is the number one in charge after Pablo was killed, I'm not sure if the beast is still on-site or not. We should assume the thing is unless someone can confirm otherwise."

He wasn't looking forward to seeing Alejandro Quintero again. The best Hal could hope for was that the man would be at the compound with the terrorists when Raina blew up the bomb.

Raina studied the map then looked up at him. "I heard about the tiger and how Pablo Sanchez used to feed his enemies to the animal."

"Yeah. I witnessed the aftermath of one of those human feasts firsthand during the last mission. Not something I want to see again. I have to say, it's going to be tough. There's a lot against us, including having to wear heavy Hazmat suits and respirators once we get to the ridge."

"And pray like hell that nothing goes wrong—like the bomb accidentally going off before we reach the ridge," Angela added.

It was a chance they would have to take. There were a lot of risks, and they all knew that. Hal didn't want any of them suited up any longer than necessary. It would be tough enough moving through the thick vegetation in the heat. "Remember, most dirty bombs have very localized effects as far as the radioactive material is concerned, ranging from less than a city block to several miles depending on a number of factors, the weather and which direction the wind is blowing. As long as we're suited up, we'll be fine."

Anticipation chomped at his veins, and he could tell everyone's nerves were on edge. He wanted to get this mission over with then go back home to his nice quiet life. He hoped this would be the last time he was in Colombia for a long time. The place reeked of death and war.

"It's also going to be hot traveling through the jungle in those suits so make sure you're well hydrated. I saw a couple cases of energy drinks in the bunker. You might want to toss a couple bottles and extra water in your backpacks."

Both women nodded.

"Do we have an exit plan?" Raina asked.

Angela handed Raina another piece of paper and passed one to Hal. "This is the best I can come up with on short notice. I had to call in a lot of favors to make this one work. There's a joint night-time anti-drug training operation funded by the Pentagon's Joint Combined Exchange Training program going on involving the US Army and the National Army of Colombia in one of the largest coca fields. They're going to be running mock raids on a narco-guerrilla camp and a cocaine lab."

"Sounds like fun," Raina said.

"If we want a way out, we have to be on that flight at exactly eight in the morning. The training exercise ends at six-thirty and we'll board as soon as the local army clears out. The helicopter will be located fifty-five kilometers west of our target's location. Arrangements have already been made. The army knows we're coming. We just have to get there.

If we don't, we're screwed, and I'll have to come up with another plan."

Hal wasn't too thrilled about Angela's plan. Too many guys with guns in one location. But they weren't in the country legally. They couldn't just fly out through a public airport. There was no way in hell they were going to ask Serigo for his help again. They'd have to take what they could get and hoped it all worked out.

"I think that's all for now." He stood and stretched his legs. "It's a sixteen-hour drive to our target so let's get loaded up and on our way."

CHAPTER EIGHT

Hal drove the Renault down the winding road and headed northeast toward Bogotá.

Raina sat quietly in the back seat and peered out the dusty window at the emerald-covered mountains rising up on both sides of the road, radiating in the bouncing glow of the headlights. They'd been traveling for almost fourteen hours straight, other than two ten-minute rest stops along the way.

At one-fifteen in the morning, the road was barren. They'd only passed three vehicles, and so far, they hadn't run into any security barricades or military checkpoints. But she knew the blockades could pop up anywhere, anytime. She glanced over her shoulder to the back loaded with weapons, suits, ammunition, drones and the XM45 covered with heavy blankets they'd taken from the safe house.

Faint gusts of wind filtered in through the open car windows. Thunder rumbled in the distance sounding like someone continuously pounding on a bass drum. The air felt cool, yet suffocating, like a gloved hand tight around her throat squeezing tighter and tighter as each minute passed. She inhaled a shaky breath and exhaled, trying to shake off the wave of panic that had been intensifying the closer they got to the area of their target.

Raina was scared—terrified the operation would fail.

The unthinkable had already happened, the attack at the nuclear plant, and it could happen again if they weren't able to stop the terrorists. It was a heavy burden for three people to deal with, a lot for Raina to deal with, the fate of so many lives resting in their hands. The deep ache in her heart that she'd experienced earlier returned. They couldn't fail. Her daughter was counting on her to return home.

Angela passed an energy bar over the seat. "Here. We all need to keep up our strength."

A hard knot formed in Raina's stomach. Right now, the last thing she wanted to do was eat. "Thanks." Even though she couldn't stomach eating, she took the protein bar and set it next to her on the seat. She looked forward to when the mission was over so she could stuff herself full of all her favorite foods and crack open the special 2003 bottle of Krug Clos du Mesnil she had been saving for a special occasion.

Defeating evil sounded like a good reason to celebrate. If she got the opportunity to kill Abdul Shakra and Alejandro Quintero, she was taking it. Nothing would give her more satisfaction, but Raina also knew how it worked. Eliminate the bad guys and quickly, others step up to replace them. It was a never-ending cycle of evil.

As they traveled up the mountain, the temperature dropped five degrees, due to the higher elevation. When they drove around a bend, she caught a whiff of coffee plant blossoms that smelled like jasmine planted in large patches up one side of the mountain.

"We're about an hour away from a dirt road the cartel used to transport cocaine out of their jungle labs. It overlooks Pablo Sanchez's old compound, the area where the bomb is supposed to be."

"Let's hope it's still there and they haven't moved it. I don't know about you two, but I don't feel like going on a wild goose chase, looking for a bomb. Not in this country," Angela said, then she lit a cigarette and took a long drag, blowing the smoke out the window.

Raina's pulse sped up. They'd be there soon.

She'd noticed the tight lines around Angela's mouth and the fine lines crinkling the woman's forehead when she spoke. She'd also noticed the only time the woman seemed to smoke was when she was nervous. Raina wasn't the only one who was skittish about what they were about to do. She picked up her backpack from the floor and unzipped the pocket then double-checked to ensure her supply of potassium iodine pills were easily accessible if needed. She'd read the information insert enclosed in the white and red package back at the safe house and knew the chemical worked quickly by saturating the thyroid, making it almost impossible for the iodine from a radioactive event to be absorbed. Instead, it would be flushed out in urine. Fingers crossed that the medicine wouldn't be needed.

Dim headlights in the distance in the opposite lane caught her attention. It had been hours since they'd seen another vehicle on this desolate road. Raina straightened and leaned forward. The seatbelt tightened against her chest. The headlights weren't getting closer. Uneasiness flowed through her body. She reached for her pistol on the seat, raked the slide back, and checked to make sure there was a round in the chamber then slipped the gun under her leg, ready to whip out if she needed to.

"I only see two." Hal slowed the Renault.

Raina spotted the barricade five-hundred yards away, blocking the road. Two men dressed in military fatigues stood on each side of the wooden barrier, holding assault rifles. She unlatched her seatbelt, not sure if they were military, police or cartel. It was hard to tell in this area of Colombia. It was anyone's guess. One of the camo-clad men walked up the road toward the car with his weapon pointed at the ground. She tightened her grip on the Beretta.

Angela passed Hal a SIG 226 with an Osprey 45 suppressor. "We don't have a choice."

Hal took the gun. "Everyone play it cool."

Angela was right. They couldn't take the chance the car might be searched, not with all the weapons and equipment in the back. If they wanted to get up the mountain to their target, they would have to take the men out. There was no other way.

Raina didn't want to be in the confined space of the car if a shootout erupted, especially with all the ammunition in the back that could explode. "Do you have that map Serigo gave you?"

Angela passed it over the seat to her. "What are you going to do?"

She leaned forward and slid her weapon in the back of her cargo pants. "Ask for directions, of course. As soon as we stop, Angela and I will get out first. Then, Hal, you get out. I'll take the guy coming toward us. Angela, you take the other one."

Angela nodded and checked her weapon.

Camo-guy held up his hand ordering them to halt.

Hal slowed the car and rolled to a stop about fifty feet from the man.

Tension filled the car.

Raina opened the door slowly and got out of the vehicle. Angela followed her lead and stayed near the passenger side door while Hal stood in between both women.

Raina waved the man over, using the map in her hand. *"Estamos perdidos. Puedes ayudarnos?"*

The man kept his one hand on the trigger of the rifle and flicked on the flashlight clutched in his other hand. He looked Hal up and down, then shone the beam of light in Raina's face. His eyes shifted to Angela.

Raina caught a glint of uncertainty in the man's eyes. He wasn't completely buying their lost routine.

"Tengo que buscar el coche primero y luego te puedo ayudar," the man said, jerking the rifle toward the ground as he spoke.

He wanted to search the car for cocaine first and then he'd help them with directions. That wasn't going to happen. Her gaze connected with Angela's, signaling it was time. Raina dropped the map.

The man stepped back and watched it flutter to the ground.

Raina's hand was on her gun before camo-guy had a chance to blink, let alone react.

A loud crack of thunder preempted the bullet that ripped through his heart, knocking him off his feet and flat onto his back in the middle of the road. A flash of jagged lightning cast a brief spotlight to illuminate the road.

Angela pulled the trigger.

A few seconds later, the man standing at the barricade dropped.

"We need to move them out of sight," Hal said, as he bent and grabbed camo-guy by the hands and dragged him off the road into the dense bushes.

Raina and Angela jogged toward the barricade. Water splashed under their shoes, and rain streamed down their faces, making it difficult for them to see. Raina stopped and spotted the man lying on his side between the barricade and the Jeep with its lights still on. She shook the water from her face.

The slug had hit him between the eyes and left a gaping hole where the bridge of his nose once was, revealing chunks of cartilage and bone. She clutched the man's arms while Angela lifted his feet. They carried him into the deep ditch behind a tree, confident he wouldn't be found for days. By that time, Raina would be home with her daughter.

Angela scrubbed the wetness from her face with her free hand. "What are we going to do with the vehicle?"

Raina clutched the dead man's rifle in her hand. She didn't want any presence of what just happened left for someone else to stumble upon and question. Not when they were so close to their target. The fewer people in the area, the fewer threats they would have to deal with. "You and Hal follow me in the car. I'll dump it higher up the mountain." She wiped the water from her eyes and squeezed the excess rain from her ponytail. "Help me lift the barricade. We'll put it in the back of the Jeep."

When they were about to move the structure, Hal pulled up in the Renault and tossed the wooden barrier in the back for them.

Raina opened the car door and turned to Hal. "Stay close. I'm going to ditch this thing."

He nodded. "We will." Then he and Angela got back into the Renault.

Raina started the engine and slammed the vehicle into gear.

A half a mile later, the road narrowed and transformed into a bumpy maze of potholes. Light from the headlights jounced and bucked off the road and into the trees. The Renault's headlights glared in the rear-view mirror a couple car lengths behind her. Ahead, she noticed the perfect spot to get rid of the Jeep.

She downshifted and came to a stop, angling the vehicle to the right, pointing the hood toward the edge of the cliff. She grabbed the assault rifle on the seat and hopped out. She moved the seat back and wedged the butt of the gun between the seat and gas pedal. She glanced over her shoulder at Hal and Angela stopped in the middle of the road and then threw the gearshift into drive. The Jeep jolted forward, its engine squealing in the rain. The vehicle fishtailed and catapulted off the side of the mountain.

Raina ran to the Renault, threw open the door, and leapt in. She wasn't waiting around, knowing the Jeep would hit solid ground and possibly create a noisy explosion on impact. She didn't want to be in the area when it happened.

As they continued up the narrowing road, the drive was harrowing between the potholes and the fact they were less than three feet from the edge of the mountain. Thick foliage scraped against the driver's side of the car, the sound unnerving. She clutched the door handle with one hand and the back of Hal's seat with the other, the seatbelt taut against her shoulder. It would take only one mistake and the car would be tumbling over the cliff, with them in it. Adrenaline built in her veins. They were almost to the site of the bomb. Raina could feel it, the undeniable shift in the air filled with anticipation and fear. She stared out the window for a long moment and said a silent prayer, begging for the chance to make it safely home to Jayden.

CHAPTER NINE

The heavy rain had stopped, the warm air fresh and disinfected as if the filth of the world had been scrubbed away. Hal crept the car along the dirt road and spotted the clearing free of impenetrable flora, leading to the ridge shadowing Pablo Sanchez's old compound. The jungle canopy was thick overhead and choked out any light coming from the moon. In the darkness, insects trilled stories back and forth while mosquitoes and gnats congregated in the glow of the headlights. After they got out of the vehicle, he opened the trunk and unloaded the boxes containing their suits and respirators. He tossed the handheld radiation detector in his backpack. A hard lump formed in his throat. He studied Raina's face in the dim light and then Angela's. Their expressions were tight and focused, their body language stiff and tense. They were scared to death.

So was Hal.

He knew when he signed on for the operation; Chambers had made it clear that the odds of then being successful sucked, let alone coming out of the mission alive. Hal was still young, fifty-one and had a lifetime ahead of him. He planned on proving the asshole wrong. He swallowed the lump and reminded himself they were the best. That's why they were chosen.

They could do this.

"Let's take a quick look around and confirm the bomb is here. Once we get to the ridge, Angela, send up the drone so we can get a better look." He glanced at the Hazmat suits and respirators. "You can put these on now or wait until we see what's happening around the compound. If you're not going to suit up now, make sure you have your backpack on at all times with your iodine tablets handy in case shit hits the fan."

"I'll wait," Angela said, her eyes shifting to Raina.

There was a brief moment of silence before Raina answered. "It'll be easier to move around without the suit on. I'll wait."

He handed the women each a mic and earpiece then attached his mic to the collar of his T-shirt and stuck the earpiece in his ear. He adjusted it so it fit snug yet comfortable and then gave it a test.

"Can you hear me?"

"Yes," the women said in unison.

"Be aware there's a small chance we might lose communications due to the radioactive material after the bomb is detonated. Keep that in mind. Stay together, no matter what."

While Raina pulled out three flashlights and handed each of them one, Hal picked up a pair of night vision binoculars. "Stay together and keep your eyes to the ground for any booby traps. I don't smell or see any smoke, so we might have gotten off lucky. Maybe there aren't any labs running tonight."

Raina tightened the straps on her backpack. "Or Alejandro Quintero got smart and shut them down while the bomb was in the cartel's backyard."

Hal figured she was probably right. Alejandro wasn't a stupid man, but as far as Hal was concerned, he would be a dead man by the time the mission was over.

When they were ready to go, Hal flicked off the headlights to ensure they wouldn't be dealing with a drained battery and miss their helicopter flight back to the US.

"So, this is where the cartel had most of their coke labs. Nice place. Secluded and close to the compound," Raina said.

Hal wiped the sweat from his forehead. "The cartel used to have one of the largest jungle laboratories up here in the country, producing millions of dollars a day worth of product, until The National Police and the Colombian Army dismantled the operation under pressure from the US. Oscar was one of the cops who helped shut it down."

Angela nodded. "I remember that. The US war on drugs. Get rid of the drugs before they come into the country."

As they plodded north toward the compound, Hal scanned the jungle floor, and the light from his flashlight swayed back and forth. With each cautious step, the earth was soft and damp beneath his feet.

Ten minutes later, he threw up his hand. His heart pounded triple-time. "Stop."

Angela and Raina halted in their tracks.

"I see it. It runs over there." Angela pointed to the right.

The tripwire, twelve-feet in length, was partially covered with dried leaves and brush.

Raina ran the beam of her flashlight along the length the wire, which appeared to end at a cluster of three giant rubber trees next to a burnt-out wooden shack.

Birds scattered and torpedoed into other treetops as if sensing danger. The reverberating flutter of leaves echoed around them.

Raina's head snapped skyward. "That was weird. Maybe they're telling us something."

Hal's muscles tensed. He hoped not. He glanced left then right, searching the darkness and didn't see anything out of the ordinary. "Yeah, really weird. Let's keep moving."

After cautiously stepping over the wire and hiking another five-hundred yards he eyed the wide opening in the vegetation, like an alley leading to the ridge. As they approached, light from the moon spilled and spread across the jungle floor lighting the way. They turned off their flashlights and kept their eyes focused on the ground in case there were any more booby traps. Hal exhaled a sigh of relief that there weren't any more, that they'd made it this far. He crouched beside the trunk of a tree and shrugged his backpack off his shoulders. From this height, he could make out the mansion on the compound grounds situated at the bottom of a huge bowl with mountains on each side. Images of the last mission flashed through his mind, in particular, the image of Oscar lying on the kitchen floor, bleeding to death. Hal shook the gruesome images from his mind and forced himself to concentrate on the task at hand.

Angela and Raina took positions on either side of him and removed their packs. While Angela was busy attaching the infrared thermal camera to the underbelly of the drone and checking the propellers and landing gear, Hal handed Raina the night vision binoculars. "We need confirmation of the bomb."

She nodded. "Let's hope it's still there."

Angela clutched the transmitter and turned on the unit. A red light blinked, and the motor fired up, followed by a green indicator light. "You're a go."

Seconds later, the drone lifted off the ground, hovered, then flew high and in the direction of the compound. Hal huddled next to her and watched images burst to life on the screen of the receiver the closer the drone got to the target area. Red, orange, and yellow heat signatures popped up and transformed into human shapes one after another along the winding foothills below.

A cloud of tiny flies swarmed around him. He waved his hand and shooed them away then continued to study the screen. "Christ, there has to be close to seventy men down there."

"That's just in the immediate area," Angela said. "They won't be there for long. Once that bomb goes off—"

"We've got confirmation." Raina lowered the binoculars and looked at Hal. "The bomb is on-site. They might be planning on moving it. I'm not sure. There's a large green army-style truck parked in the driveway on the west side of the house with the back door open—about twenty men are standing around it."

Angela piloted the drone and kept an eye on the receiver's screen. The device circled and then came back and flew behind them.

Sweat broke out across Hal's hairline at the gentle tremble in Raina's voice and the fear lurking behind her eyes.

This was about to get real.

"Do you see Quintero or Abdul Shakra?"

There was a long pause before she answered. "No."

He definitely heard the disappointment in Raina's voice. He wasn't the only one who planned to kill the men if given the chance.

The dim white LED lights of the drone shone above and hovered. Angela thumbed the remote-control stick. The device lowered slowly and landed a foot in front of her. She quickly disassembled the unit and returned everything to her backpack. "I counted another twenty-five on the east side of the compound about a half mile up the road. Looks like a convoy."

Hal stood and cursed to himself. Hopefully, it was a convoy that escorted the bomb to the compound and not the other way around. "We'd better head back to the car and get suited up in case they are planning on moving out." He looked at Angela and Raina and had a hard time getting the words out. "This is it. Operation Oblivion is about to begin."

CHAPTER TEN

Raina was shaking from the inside out. There was something terrifying about wearing a Hazmat suit. She zipped up the black full body suit, her skin tingling and slick with wetness. The protective gear had better be top of the line. Otherwise, she'd hunt down Serigo and jab a knife in his other thigh. For a moment she wondered if rodent-face had paid his debt and gotten his niece back. She prayed he had. Then her thoughts shifted to her daughter, and a wave of melancholy washed over her. Right now, more than anything she wanted to hear Jayden say, "Momma."

I'll be home soon, baby.

They'd get rid of the bomb then be on their way to the helicopter and out of Colombia. With any luck, she'd be home later tonight reading her daughter a bedtime story. She couldn't wait.

"We're going to melt in these things." Angela frowned and continued pulling the suit up over her waist. "Damn thing is sticking to my skin."

The woman looked like a ninja warrior wearing a loose-fitting scuba-like wet suit. Hal did too. She had to admit the gear was hot and uncomfortable. She took the last sip of an energy drink, determined not to end up dehydrated and tossed the bottle at her feet.

"We'll only be suited up for as long as we have to be. We don't know how much nuclear material they've used in the bomb. We also don't know the quantity or the type of explosives used. Remember, the moment the Z45 is fired, everyone hit to the ground. Keep your heads down and do not watch the explosion. We've only got five seconds between firing and impact."

Angela nodded and slipped her feet into a pair of black protective boots.

Raina noticed how Angela's head shook slightly. The woman already had smoked her 'nervous' cigarette, savoring it as if it was her last. Hal appeared calm, but his face told a different story, the way his brows drew together and the lines at the corners of his eyes seemed more pronounced in the moonlight.

Everyone's nerves were on the brink, fearing the unknown. It's not as if they had detonated a dirty bomb before. They were in foreign territory with a long list of unknowns. It was going to be difficult to move around freely wearing the suit, gloves, masks, and boots, but she'd rather be over protected than not covered enough. She'd figure it out and make it work.

Hal grabbed the bolt action .300 Win Mag sniper rifle complete with a Nightforce NXS 8-32x56 scope and swivel biopad out of the trunk.

She knew he wanted to kill Alejandro and Abdul if they were at the compound. It was exactly what she would do. Both were terrorists. They'd been killing and terrorizing for decades. She was positive the Syrian government would be thrilled to see Abdul dead, just like his brother. And Raina was confident the Colombians would be pleased if Alejandro simply disappeared off the face of the earth.

After she finished suiting up, she put on her backpack and lifted the black rectangular case containing the X45 out of the back of the car.

Angela chose a Sig Sauer M400 semi-automatic rifle. She winked at Raina and wiggled her backpack on her body. "Just in case we run into any problems on the way. It's better than my handgun."

With their respirators, a flashlight in their hands, and their weapons of choice in the other, it was time. There was a silent pact in Hal's eyes, words unsaid. Raina had seen it before during other missions. It was a "let's get it done then go home" look.

As they trudged slowly through the clearing laden down with equipment and trepidation, the air felt cool against Raina's face. Beams of light from their flashlights swung like giant pendulums sweeping the ground ahead. Hal and Angela remained quiet, clearly deep in thought about what was about to happen.

With each heavy step, foliage on the jungle floor snapped and crunched under Raina's feet, and her shoulders ached from the weight of the overloaded backpack. An incessant buzz from a swarm of mosquitoes settled in a cloud around her head. Several sets of eyes twinkled in the greenery, peeking down from the tree tops.

Her heart stopped.

Everyone halted.

"What is it?" Angela asked, her voice almost a whisper.

Hal shone his flashlight in the direction of the glaring eyes. "It's just monkeys."

The white-faced howler monkeys screeched to each other then jumped to other branches overhead.

Moments later, relief flooded Raina's body after they successfully dodged a tripwire for the second time. Ahead, she spotted the lit opening in the jungle canopy. Her pulse sped up.

Once they were at the ridge, they removed their backpacks and set them beside them for easy access in case something happened, and they needed the iodine tablets. Angela lay on her stomach between Raina and Hal with the strap of her respirator clutched in her hand.

Below, the compound was well lit. Dozens of men clustered in pockets of three or four around the pool and at the back of the house next to the truck.

Hal got down on his knees and lay flat, positioning the sniper rifle in front of him. He looked through the scope. "Shit. I don't see Quintero or Shakra. Maybe they're not here."

Raina knew Abul Shakra well. There was no way he'd allow the bomb out of his sight. "I can't imagine either man not being on-site. We're talking about very expensive cargo they have on the truck. I can guarantee both men are somewhere close, probably barking orders to each other."

"Well, if they're inside the house, they're going to get a huge wake-up call when the bomb explodes," Angela said.

Hal moved the sniper rifle to his right. He looked at Raina and pulled the hood on his suit over his head. "You ready?"

No. Panic choked her, like a dozen strong hands around her throat, and her limbs froze for a few seconds. Her eyes darted to Angela and then back to Hal. She gave a quick nod, unable to speak and flipped the latches on the X45 case and opened it, her gloved hands visibly shaking. She yanked up her hood then put the respirator over her face, tightening the straps around her head. She inhaled a shaky breath and exhaled, her breath moist and warm inside the respirator, and looked down at Hal and Angela one last time geared up from head to toe.

Raina raised the X45 and peered through the scope. She swallowed hard and bit back fear.

After activating the laser rangefinder, the weapon automatically calculated the distance between her and the truck. She clicked the incremental button near the trigger and adjusted the detonating distance adding three meters to cover the length of the truck.

Her heart thumped. Sweat pooled and dripped inside the suit and ran down her neck. The indicator locked on the target at twenty-two-hundred feet.

Raina pulled the trigger.

One...

She dropped to the ground, rolled on her stomach, and covered her head with her hands. She squeezed her eyes shut. Jayden's face flashed through her mind.

Two...

Three...

Four...

A deafening bang.

The earth rocked below her and vibrated through her limbs. For a moment, her mind and body went numb.

The blast wave rushed overhead like a roaring tornado, stripping branches and searing off the tops of trees. Dirt and twigs pelted her suit. Raina clawed at the strap of her backpack and held on to it with all her strength. The supersonic wall of air uprooted plants and small bushes and decimated the vegetation in its wake then vacuumed back toward the source of the explosion.

Her eyepiece crackled. Then went silent.

She turned her head toward Angela and opened her eyes.

The woman was staring at her, wide eyed with shock.

"Is—everyone—okay?" Hal asked.

Raina was relieved when she heard his voice in her ear, even though it sounded like he was talking underwater.

She climbed to one knee and stayed there for a moment, feeling a bit disoriented and dizzy. "Yes."

"I'm—okay," Angela said in a small strained voice. She slowly rose to her feet and wobbled. Hal grabbed her arm and steadied her.

When Raina finally got her bearings, she lumbered to her feet and peered over the ridge.

Thick gray and white plumes of smoke mushroomed toward the stars. The night sky was bright from the brilliant orange and red flames engulfing the house and garage. The truck carrying the bomb was gone—disintegrated. Dozens of vehicles that were parked in the driveway earlier were empty twisted metal shells.

Small spotty fires dotted the grass around the swimming pool and raced up the palm trees. The burning leaves looked like lit candles waving in the wind. Most of the brick house and garage were gone as if someone had chiseled out the top three-quarters of both structures.

If Quintero or Shakra were inside the house when the bomb exploded, they were dead. There was no way anyone in the immediate area of the blast could have survived.

"We need to get out of here and get to the car. The area will be teeming with police and military once the news gets out that something happened." Hal picked up his backpack and handed Angela hers. The sniper rifle and the XM45 were long gone, sucked up in the vacuum of the explosion.

Raina slowly lifted her heavy pack and swung it over one shoulder, too exhausted and sore to put it on properly. As they walked back to the Renault, a headache pounded behind her eyes and her mouth was dry as dirt. They were all probably dehydrated. Hopefully, once they were far enough away from the explosion site, they'd be able to remove the respirators and re-hydrate. They did it and survived. Now all they had to do was drive fifty-five miles west to the helicopter. Then she would be on her way home to her daughter. She couldn't wait.

Fifteen minutes later, they were in the car. Relief filled her body. She sat in the passenger seat and leaned her head on the headrest. Angela sat in the back with their backpacks stacked next to her. Everyone was quiet, likely still processing what they had done.

Hal rammed the key in the ignition and turned. The engine fired up then shut off. He slammed his hand down on the steering wheel. "Shit."

"The radioactive particles must have messed with the electric system," Angela said. "This can't be happening. We need to get out of here. We can't get caught."

Within the hour the place would be crawling with military and cartel. They needed to exit the area before it was locked down. Panic quickly replaced the relief she'd felt moments ago. Suddenly, it felt as if a cement block was sitting on Raina's chest. She inhaled and exhaled long deep breaths and forced her breathing and heart rate to calm.

Hal started the car. The motor spit and chugged, and then died.

Angela leaned forward between the seats. "What are we going to do?"

"We'll have to wait a little longer and try again. We don't have a choice."

Raina looked at Hal. "We probably don't have much time."

"I know."

Minutes ticked by like hours.

Raina was hot. Her skin and clothes were drenched with sweat, making it difficult to move with the suit on. She shifted in the seat, trying to find a comfortable position but failed. The longer she was stuck in the suit and respirator, the more she felt trapped—and she didn't like it.

"Let's try this again." Hal turned the key. The engine growled to life. "Come on. Stay running."

The motor purred and continued running.

"Amen," Angela howled.

Raina's thoughts exactly. She expelled the breath she realized she had been holding. Operation Oblivion was over. They'd won—this time around.

Hal threw the car into drive and steered down the narrow dirt path to the main road, then drove west.

CHAPTER ELEVEN

At five-forty, rays of light sparked ribbons of pink and orange across the horizon. As Hal continued to drive west, dark rolling hills on both sides of the road transformed into vibrant green vegetation in the early morning light. He glanced in the rear-view mirror, and then to the side mirror, happy to see no one following them. In about twenty minutes, they would be at the site of the joint mock raids then on the helicopter heading home to the US.

Hal glanced at Raina sitting next to him with her gloved hands resting in her lap. Both women had to be mentally and physically exhausted. Going through an explosion like that was tough on the body and the mind.

He still couldn't believe they'd destroyed a radioactive bomb. He had no idea what type of explosives the terrorists had used, but it was one of the strongest blasts he'd experienced in a long time. The last time was when he was in the Marines, part of the multinational peacekeeping force in Beirut. He witnessed a truck filled with two-and-a-half-tons of explosives smash into a building where three-hundred Marines were sleeping, killing two-hundred and forty-one American service members.

His muscles ached and sweat ran down the back of his neck and chest. They needed to get this hot gear off. They were far enough away from the blast zone, and from what he could tell, the wind was blowing southeast, away from them. He looked in the rear-view mirror and noticed Angela staring out the side window. She'd been so quiet he thought she had fallen asleep.

"Donahue. Can you grab the radiation detector from my backpack? We need to see if we can get out of these damn suits and get some fluids into us. We need to."

"Gladly. Right now, my body feels like lead. I think we're all pretty dehydrated."

Raina straightened her legs and repositioned herself in the seat. "My muscles are beginning to cramp up."

"We'll find some place to pull over. We still have plenty of time to get to the helicopter location."

A mile later, Hal steered the Renault off the main road into what appeared to be an old deserted driveway with an abundance of overgrown weeds that opened up to a grassy area. They rolled to a stop a few yards away from a cluster of wax palm trees. He kept the engine running, not wanting to take any chances it might not start again.

Hal and Raina got out of the car. He could tell by the way she was moving, slowly and stiffly, that the muscles in her legs had cramped up pretty badly.

"You okay?"

Raina nodded. "I'll be okay."

He knew she wasn't by the way her face twisted in pain with each spasm.

Angela stumbled out of the back seat and steadied herself with the car door then tossed their backpacks one by one out onto the ground. "It would be nice to breathe fresh air. Here." She handed him the small black rectangular device.

Hal turned on the unit, then flicked the switch marked 'air'. He watched the LED screen light up, wishing he could wipe away the sweat that was running down his temples and along his chin under the respirator. A red light blinked and chirped with each count as it updated the numbers every few seconds.

Raina glanced at him, her face glistening with moisture behind the face-shield of the respirator. "How long does it take?"

"We should probably let it run for at least a half-hour. Don't have the time, though. We'll give it five, maybe ten minutes. That's about all we can spare. Afterward, we should test the inside of the car to make sure there aren't any high-levels of radiation from any particles that might be on our suits."

The sun beat down on Hal's back and made him sweat even more. The alarm on the detector hadn't gone off so far, which was a good thing. Five minutes passed, and the unit let out a long high-pitched beep. A yellow light blinked then turned to solid green, indicating the air was within an acceptable radiation level.

"According to this thing, we're safe. Get these damn things off, respirators last. If you want to change into dry clothes, do it now because we need to head out soon."

Angela sat on the ground and pulled off her rubber boots. "Thank God."

"Might be a good idea to take the tablets, just in case. Remember where the detector came from." Raina peeled off her gloves, and then yanked her boots and threw them into the bushes.

Hal nodded. Serigo had bought the detector on the black market. 'Serigo' and the word 'trust'. Two things he was uneasy with. "Good idea."

He had never seen three people remove protective gear and change into dry clothing so quickly. When they were done, Hal checked the radiation levels inside the car and exhaled a huge sigh of relief when the green beeping light stayed on.

After downing two energy drinks each and agreeing they should all take the iodine tablets, they loaded back into the Renault. Hal backed up the car and wheeled the vehicle onto the main road.

"I'm guessing the word is out by now." Raina turned on the radio and flipped through the stations, but the only sound that came out of the radio was either dead silence or crackling.

For the next fifteen minutes, no one said a word. Fresh warm air rushed in and circulated throughout the car. Two motorcycles whizzed by followed by a powder blue Renault.

Hal looked over at Raina. "Feeling better?"

"Definitely. Makes me want to never be suited up again." She took a sip of water then ripped open an energy bar and took a bite.

"How are you doing, Angela?"

"Better now. I'm with Raina. No more missions requiring protective gear."

He laughed. It was one of the most difficult missions he'd been involved with. He didn't want to ever do it again.

Raina pointed to the other lane. "Look."

Hal's muscles tightened when he spotted the long convoy of Colombian police and army vehicles. A helicopter flew in the distance and flew south.

"They must be coming from the mock raids and are heading to the explosion site."

One by one, cars, trucks and Jeeps zoomed by. He kept his eyes on the road not wanting to look too nosy or to give anyone a reason to stop them. "There was enough of them." He watched in the side mirror as the last Jeep drove past.

"There's our helicopter. We're going home, kids," Angela said.

Hal heard the excitement in her voice and smiled to himself. Then he checked his watch. They were early.

To the right, the valley was filled with row after row of four-meter-high coca plants with tapered oval green leaves. In the middle of the crop sat a US Army Bell UH-1H helicopter with four US Army soldiers standing in front of it.

Raina straightened in the seat. "We should pull over on the other side of the valley and hike back through the coca field. I counted two men wearing Colombian National Army fatigues standing about a thousand yards from our ride. Looks like they're patroling the area."

"We'll try to slip around them." Hal slowed the car, pulled over to the side of the road, and shut off the vehicle.

After they exited the car, he opened the back and grabbed the SIG 226.

Raina snatched the Beretta MA91 and folding tactical knife. She shoved the gun in the waistband of her cargo pants and popped the knife in her pocket.

Angela picked up a Jericho 941 and slipped the weapon into the back pocket of her jeans.

They ran up along the ditch until they reached the fringes of the coca field. Keeping their heads low, they zig-zagged between the rows, hard branches scratching at their arms. Hal stopped and peeked through the plants. "Circle around to the back of the helicopter. Keep your head down."

Raina and Angela nodded then rushed through the plants toward the helicopter.

Hal turned.

The barrel of an assault rifle was shoved in his face.

His pulse thudded in his ears. He looked up at Colombian camo-guy and cursed to himself for getting caught.

The man directed with his rifle for Hal to stand up.

Out of the corner of his eye, he spotted Raina sneaking down the row behind camo-guy. Within seconds, she kicked the man in the back of the knees and had him pinned on the ground with a knife stuck in the side of his neck.

"Thanks." Hal pulled out his weapon. "Where's Angela?"

"She should be at the helicopter by now."

"Alto!"

Hal poked his head above the plants.

Camo-guy number two had his AK-47 aimed at Angela's back.

Two of the US soldiers had their weapons trained on camo-guy.

Hal turned to Raina. She was gone. Disappearing seemed to be a bad habit of hers.

A gunshot pierced the air.

Camo-guy dropped to the ground.

Raina emerged from the field, two-handing her gun, her ponytail swinging in the wind. She ran and grabbed Angela's hand, and they darted for the chopper.

The helicopter's engine powered up.

Whump-Whump-Whump.

Hal lowered and sprinted along the row of coca. The downdraft of the main rotor roared a blast of typhoon-force air around him, spitting a whirlwind of leaves and dust. Shielding his eyes from the debris, he jumped into the helicopter just as the chopper's landing skids bounced then lifted off the ground.

The chopper's blades sliced into the sky and veered to the right then flew in a wide circle.

He glanced at Angela and Raina sitting in one of the bench seats in the back across from the other soldiers. Raina smiled, and Angela gave him a 'thumbs-up'.

The pilot handed him a headset.

He leaned back in the seat and put it on.

"Glad you could make it. You know we're probably not going to get invited back for another training mission with the Colombians," the pilot said.

Hal laughed. "That's okay. We sure as hell don't want to come back again, either."

CHAPTER TWELVE

Four days later…

Jayden ran down the hallway, her bare feet thumping on the wood floor. "Momma!"

Raina looked at her daughter. "What, baby?"

"Look." Jayden spun around, wearing a yellow skirt with black pants and a hot pink T-shirt that she had on backwards and inside out.

"You dressed yourself. Good job. You look beautiful. Why don't you go and color? I put your favorite coloring book on the kitchen table."

"I'm beautiful." Jayden grinned and skipped toward the kitchen.

Raina turned at Hal and Angela sitting on the couch. "She's been a bit wound up since I got home."

"She loves you a lot. She's thrilled you're home," Angela said.

Her daughter wasn't the only one. Raina was happy to be back. She'd missed Jayden more than anyone would know. The look on her daughter's face when Raina walked through the door of the safe house was imprinted in her mind. She'd never seen the little girl so excited. It had taken Raina hours to settle the child down.

"You going somewhere?" Hal asked.

Raina's eyes shifted to the boxes stacked against the living room wall that she planned on putting in storage, and then back to Hal.

They were flying to Bangkok tomorrow morning and staying with a friend until she could find a suitable and safe place. She and Jayden needed to get out of the US after what had happened at the nuclear plant.

"If you two found me, and Abdul Shakra's men were able to find me to, it's time for us to move on. My daughter's safety comes first. Always will."

"That's understandable. We finally got an ID on the men who were sent to kill you. Barir Farhat and Jaul Rahaim. Two of Abdul Shakra's trusted hit squad. The guy you duct taped to the pole is Ra'id Touma, some low-life radical, looking to be an ISIS wanna-a-be. They'll spend some time in jail. Who knows? Maybe afterward, they'll disappear."

She understood what Hal was saying. Someone would make sure the men disappeared. Probably a good thing because they'd find a way to come after her again, and next time she might not be so lucky. But in the end, it didn't matter if they were out of the picture or not. There would always be someone resolute on making her pay for her past with the CIA.

"We don't have confirmation yet if Alejandro Quintero and Abdul Shakra were killed at the compound. Colombian news sources are only reporting there was a large explosion. No mention of a dirty bomb. Or reports of any radiation."

That didn't surprise Raina since half of the country was on the cartel's payroll. The blast would be downplayed, and any news coming out of the country would be censored. It would take three to six months for the truth to come out...if it ever did.

She peeked around the corner to the kitchen. Jayden was still busy at the table coloring. "Do you guys think they're dead?"

Angela nodded.

"More than likely," Hal said.

She hoped they were right. "Please thank Robson and Russler again for me. I'm grateful they kept my daughter safe."

"We will." Angela crossed her legs. "We did learn this morning that all future joint missions between the US and Colombia have been suspended."

That news didn't surprise Raina, either. It didn't look good when two Colombian soldiers were killed with a US chopper a thousand yards away.

"Have you spoken to Serigo?" Hal asked.

She had called rodent-face, and he apologized a dozen times for demanding more money. "I talked to him yesterday. He paid his debt and got his niece back. She's safe. He said he was thinking of moving his whole family to Brazil, away from the Nino's Ricos gang. I think he learned his lesson." At least, she hoped he had.

"That's good," Angela said. "Happy to know his niece is okay."

"Yeah. Glad it worked out for him. I still don't trust the guy," Hal said as he stood. "Well, we should get going."

Angela rose from the couch and hugged her. "We did a good thing. Probably saved a lot of lives. Thanks for saving my life."

Raina smiled.

Angela released her and glanced over at Hal. "I'll meet you out front."

After Angela left, Hal handed Raina a white card. "If you ever get in trouble and you need help, call me. I mean that. Angela and I have a lot of contacts and resources at our disposal. Probably not as many as you do. Just in case."

"Thanks." She took the card.

Hal touched her arm. "Enjoy your daughter, Raina, because she'll grow up way too fast." Then he turned and walked out the door.

Raina stood at the living room window and watched the silver SUV back out of the driveway. Sadness tugged at her heart. She actually liked Hal and Angela. But part of her hoped she would never see them again. If she did, they probably needed her help and she didn't want to have to say no.

Author's Note

I hope you enjoyed reading *Dawn of the Storm*. The book was a blast to write.

To my fans, readers, and reviewers—thank you! You rock!

The story was originally published in 2015 featuring JET from Russell Blake's *New York Times* and *USA Today* bestselling action thriller series. The story was recently reworked with a new kick-ass character, Raina Storm, who will also be appearing in the fourth Whitney Steel romantic thriller: *Redemption*.

Read an excerpt from *Dawn of the Enemy* (A Raina Storm Thriller – Book Two)

Watch for *Dawn of the Red Fire*, the third book in the Raina Storm series coming soon!

DAWN OF THE ENEMY

A Raina Storm Thriller – Book Two

Kim Cresswell

KC Publishing
Ontario, Canada

KC Publishing
London, Ontario Canada

Publisher's Note: This is a work of fiction. Names, characters, places, and incidents are a product of the author's imagination. Locales and public names are sometimes used for atmospheric purposes. Any resemblance to actual people, living or dead, or to businesses, companies, events, institutions, or locales is completely coincidental.

Cover Art © 2018

Ordering Information:
Quantity sales. Special discounts are available on quantity purchases by corporations, associations, and others. For details, contact the publisher at the address above.

Dawn of the Enemy/Kim Cresswell. – 1st edition.
ISBN 978-0-9950578-9-0

CHAPTER ONE

Bangkok, Thailand

Raina Storm clutched her daughter's hand, the six-year-old's skin warm against hers, and steered through the mob of shoppers in Yaowarat, Bangkok's two-hundred-year-old Chinatown district. In the distance, bells rang, the elegant donging evoking the gods and keeping the evil forces at bay, or so the locals believed. As they strolled by one of the many street food stalls selling Pad Thai, boat noodles and suckling pig, the savory sweet smell of curry, cardamom and other delicate spices mingled around them.

Jayden pinched her nose. "Phew, Momma. That stinks."

Raina smiled and wondered if her child would ever get used to the cultural differences, let alone the banquet of Thai food she refused to eat. Sweat pooled and trickled down between her shoulder blades, her skin slick with wetness under her army green tank top. She glanced at her watch. It was one in the afternoon, the February heat unbearable, and it would only get worse as the day progressed. Dozens of pumpkin orange and gold-foiled paper lanterns hung above on wires and swayed and rustled in the stifling hot breeze, sounding like crumpled cellophane.

"Momma. Look!" Jayden's big round eyes lit up, and she pointed to a towering pyramid-shaped display of fruit at one of the vendor stalls.

She eyed the apples and bananas, her daughter's favorites. "Finally, we found something *you* will eat."

Jayden pushed her tousled bangs out of her eyes and giggled.

After paying one hundred and sixty baht in coins for fruit for her daughter and dragon fruit for herself, Raina adjusted her black leather shoulder bag, ready to get out of the heat and go home. Jayden's brown hair flopped in the wind as she skipped beside her, humming an unrecognizable song, oblivious to the heat or anything else.

They'd been living in a furnished, air-conditioned two-bedroom condominium for the past three months after leaving the US following the catastrophic attack at the Diablo Canyon Nuclear Plant, the deadliest act of terrorism since 9/11. After the attack, Raina had helped destroy a dirty bomb in Colombia before the same terrorist cell working with the *Sur del Calle* cartel could transport the device into the US and detonate it. Their plan? To take out another nuclear facility. As if one strike wasn't enough. The devastation would last for decades. Luckily, the bad guys had failed the second time around.

She hadn't signed on for the mission, instead was blackmailed into 'lending a hand' if she didn't want to see her daughter taken away and placed in a foster home. It all worked out in the end. The terrorists were dead, and the death toll had included some of the cartel's major players. Another deadly situation defused. She wasn't naive enough to think more attacks weren't coming, but for now, she felt safe in Bangkok, away from the fallout on the west coast of the United States.

She glanced over her shoulder and observed two muscular Asian men dressed in tight fitting black T-shirts and jeans strutting twenty yards behind her, their black hair glistening in the sunlight. It was their body language, the way they moved with purpose and commitment that caught her eye. The hairs on the back of her neck rose. They didn't look like the type of men who wanted to have a friendly chit-chat.

This can't happen now. Not when she was with her daughter.

Raina had seen it before. Too many times. Somehow, her past always found a way to catch up with her. She also knew it would be just a matter of time before others would show up. They always did. Concern swirled inside her. She didn't know who the men were but could only guess they were connected to one of her past assignments with the CIA, or someone else she had angered along the way. She wasn't planning on sticking around to find out. She tightened her grip on Jayden's hand and hastily weaved through the frenzy of shoppers and tourists, determined to lose her newly acquired followers.

"Too fast, Momma."

"I know, baby." Raina stopped and picked Jayden up, balancing the child on her hip before quickening her pace. "We need to hurry so you can have some bananas and juice."

Jayden smiled and wrapped her arms around

Raina's neck.

Raina glanced over her shoulder again. The men were still trailing them. She needed to lose them.

As she rushed through the dizzying maze of trinket, jewelry, and fabric vendors thronged with shoppers haggling over prices. Chinese signage in brilliant shades of pink, yellow and red creaked in the wind, the sound unnerving. She made a quick right, leaving the mob of bargain hunters behind, and jogged down a long narrow alley. She threw a final look over her shoulder. The two men closed in on her. The familiar pop of a suppressed 9mm Glock sounded much like a firecracker going off.

The sound startled Jayden, and she began to cry.

She held her daughter tight and ducked. "It's okay. Hang on, sweetie."

A slug whistled past Raina's head and thumped into a stack of broken wooden crates. She veered right and bolted, the soles of her leather sandals pounding the hot pavement.

Another pop. Then another.

She sprinted around a corner and spotted a large metal garbage bin ahead, outside the back door of a restaurant. She picked up her speed, determined to put some distance between her and her attackers.

A half a block later, her legs burned. Raina came to an abrupt stop, placed Jayden on the ground, and pulled her behind the bin. "I need you to stay right here." She lowered her voice, almost to a whisper. "Stay very quiet, and don't move even if you hear something really scary. Okay? Promise?"

Fear, confusion, and tears filled her daughter's eyes. She nodded slowly and crouched, resting her small hands on her knees.

A dog barked. Aggressive car horns honked, the sound coming from the main street.

"Momma will be right back." Raina dropped her shoulder bag next to her daughter then ran back in the direction of her attackers. She flattened her body against one of the buildings and waited.

The men had guts, unloading their weapons in broad daylight, especially in such a busy tourist area surrounded by majestic religious temples. They even had more guts, thinking they could get away with scaring her daughter.

She swiped the sweat from her eyes. This was the last thing she wanted to do in front of Jayden, but there was no other option. She was sick of spending her life always looking over her shoulder because of her past. It was like a large toxic cloud, dictating every decision in her life, and right now, protecting her daughter was first and foremost. Whoever these men were, they needed to be stopped.

Thudding footsteps approached.

She inhaled a deep breath and exhaled. Perspiration dripped from the tip of her pony-tail and slid down her back, chilling her body.

The first man crept past her, his Colt .45 aimed and readied as he headed in the direction where Jayden was hidden. The second man was nowhere in sight.

Raina ran.

Six long strides and her right foot struck the wall first. She sprinted up the side of the brick building, leapt into the air and side-kicked the gun from the man's hand with such impact it broke his arm. The brutal force of the blow slammed him to the ground. He lay on his side, dazed for a long moment then clutched his fractured and useless appendage.

She grabbed his gun and stood in front of him with the barrel of the weapon trained at his head. Her breath came out in short, forceful rasps. "Who are you?"

The man's features twisted with pain. He clenched his teeth and shook his head.

She could almost read the man's mind by the look of surprise in the back of his eyes as he realized he'd just been taken down by a woman who weighed a hundred and twenty pounds.

Raina jabbed the weapon in his forehead and held it there, a reminder she wasn't playing games. "One last time. Who are you and who sent you?"

He stared at her with fierce dark eyes, as if calculating his next move. A small smile curled the corners of his mouth. He shook his head again.

She pressed the barrel into his skin hard enough to leave an indent. "If you move, you're dead."

Another pop.

A bullet hissed past her ear, too close for comfort.

She jumped out of the line of fire and observed the second man zig-zagging through the alley. He looked like an enforcer, overly ripped, his neck the size of his upper thigh. He stopped and ducked behind a discarded wooden door, the top of his large head visible enough for her to get off a clean shot. Then Raina heard her daughter's gentle sobs. Her eyes instinctively snapped to the bin where Jayden safely tucked away, out of harm's way. The child was terrified. *Hang on, baby. Just a few more minutes.* Guilt flooded her body and her heart squeezed. This was not a situation she wanted her daughter to witness.

Out of the corner of her eye, she caught movement beside her. The man wasn't going to stay down, apparently determined to fulfill a death wish. She would be more than happy to oblige if it meant keeping her daughter safe.

She whirled and confronted her assailant.

He bounced to his feet and lunged at her.

Her heart rate accelerated. Raw adrenaline shot through her veins, and she fired the weapon.

The bullet penetrated his left eye and bored into his brain, leaving the left side of his skull shattered. His body jerked then fell backwards. What was left of his head bounced like a rubber ball against the ground then finally lopped to one side while his hand lifelessly clung to his weapon.

Raina crouched next to the body and watched Enforcer-guy moving closer, using whatever he could find tossed in the alley to help shield himself.

This time, she wasn't asking questions first.

She stood and scrambled to the corner of the building, the handle of the Colt .45 gripped tight in her hand.

This needed to end as quickly and quietly as possible. She had to get back to Jayden. The longer they were in the alley the more likely someone would stumble upon them and contact the authorities—trouble Raina didn't want or need.

She poked her head around the corner. Sweat stung her eyes and slid down the sides of her face. She blinked.

Enforcer-guy fired.

A round buzzed past and drilled into something behind her with a hollow clunk.

She held her breath and stepped out from the

corner with her gun ready.

The man decided to run to the other side of the alley but didn't get far. Her shot to the side of his neck stopped him dead in his tracks. Blood sprayed and showered down around him. He fell in a crumpled pile, his legs splayed crudely out around him as if broken.

Relieved it was over, Raina exhaled and tucked the Colt .45 in the back of the waistband of her shorts and covered it with her tank top. She would have to make a brief stop at the apartment and grab her burner cell phones, their passports, her emergency stash of cash and the gun she'd purchased for twenty-three hundred US dollars on the black market in Khlong Thom, where you could buy anything from fake passports to AK-47 rifles. It was a dangerous move to go to the apartment, but a necessary one. She also didn't have anyone in Bangkok she could trust to look after her daughter. Checking into a hotel, for now, was her only option, at least until she could figure out who was after her.

After quickly searching both bodies and collecting two wallets, Raina ran back to Jayden. As she approached, her daughter's sobs grew louder. The thought of Jayden upset made her feel even worse about what she had been forced to do. She stopped, and her eyes shifted to the ground. A thin stream of blood snaked out from behind the bin.

Raina's heart stopped, and fear froze her limbs. "Jayden!"

About the Author

Kim Cresswell resides in Ontario, Canada and is the award-winning author of the action-packed WHITNEY STEEL series.

Her romantic thriller, **Reflection** (A Whitney Steel Novel - Book One) has won numerous awards: RomCon®'s 2014 Readers' Crown Finalist (Romantic Suspense), InD'tale Magazine 2014 Rone Award Finalist (Suspense/Thriller), UP Authors Fiction Challenge Winner, Silicon Valley's Romance Writers of America (RWA) "Gotcha!" Romantic Suspense Winner, and an Honorable Mention in Calgary's (RWA) The Writer's Voice Contest.

Kim recently signed a 3-book German translation deal with LUZIFER-Verlag for the first three books in the Whitney Steel series: **Reflection**, **Retribution,** and **Resurrect**. The popular series will be published in German beginning in 2018/2019.

The Assassin Chronicles TV series, based on Kim's upcoming 4-book paranormal/supernatural thriller series: **Deadly Shadow** (May 2018)**, Invisible Truth, Assassin's Prophecy**, and **Vision of Fire** is in development with Council Tree Productions.

www.kimcresswell.ca

www.facebook.com/KimCresswellBooks

http://twitter.com/kimcresswell

Also by Kim Cresswell

Whitney Steel Series
Reflection
Retribution
Resurrect

The Assassin Chronicles Series
Deadly Shadow

Raina Storm Series
Dawn of the Storm
Dawn of the Enemy

Single Title Novellas
Lethal Journey

True Crime Short Stories
Real Life Evil
Murder on Sunset Strip
Garden of Bones
Edge of Madness

**'True Crime Anthologies Published by
Grinning Man Press**
Serial Killer Quarterly "21st Century Psychos"
Serial Killer Quarterly "Partners in Pain"
Serial Killer Quarterly "Unsolved in North
America"
Serial Killer Quarterly "Cruel Britannia"
Serial Killer Quarterly "They Almost Got Away"
Serial Killer Quarterly "Lostmord: Murder in
German"